"Brace yourself!" Gus shouted.

Jane grabbed the armrest and held on. Gus jammed on the brakes, bringing the SUV to a skidding stop. The driver behind him was too late to stop before slamming into the back of their vehicle. Gus hit the accelerator, racing ahead.

Jane glanced back to see that the other vehicle wasn't moving. Her heartbeat slowed and she took a breath. She stared across at Gus. "You've got a gunshot wound."

"I'm fine. It just grazed me."

"Grazing doesn't bleed that much." She searched for something to stop the flow of blood. When she couldn't find anything, she pressed her palm against the wound, applying pressure. "Seriously, you're bleeding like a stuck pig. You should go get some stitches."

"When we get to the estate, I'll ask for a Band-Aid."

Jane sighed. "You're hopeless."

He shot her a grin. "And you're doing great. Most women I've known would have fainted at the sight of blood."

"I'm not most women," she grumbled.

His grin faded, b⬚⬚⬚⬚⬚⬚⬚⬚⬚⬚⬚⬚⬚⬚⬚'re not…"

DRIVING FORCE

New York Times Bestselling Author

ELLE JAMES

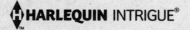

I dedicate this book to Sweetpea, a good dog who gave me lots of
love and companionship for thirteen years. For one so small,
you were a big part of my life and heart. I hope you're running
free and eating all the good treats across the rainbow bridge.
I will miss you so very much.

ISBN-13: 978-1-335-60463-7

Driving Force

Recycling programs
for this product may
not exist in your area.

Copyright © 2019 by Mary Jernigan

www.Harlequin.com

Printed in U.S.A.

Elle James, a *New York Times* bestselling author, started writing when her sister challenged her to write a romance novel. She has managed a full-time job and raised three wonderful children, and she and her husband even tried ranching exotic birds (ostriches, emus and rheas). Ask her, and she'll tell you what it's like to go toe-to-toe with an angry 350-pound bird! Elle loves to hear from fans at ellejames@earthlink.net or ellejames.com.

Books by Elle James

Harlequin Intrigue

Declan's Defenders

Marine Force Recon
Show of Force
Full Force
Driving Force

Mission: Six

One Intrepid SEAL
Two Dauntless Hearts
Three Courageous Words
Four Relentless Days
Five Ways to Surrender
Six Minutes to Midnight

Ballistic Cowboys

Hot Combat
Hot Target
Hot Zone
Hot Velocity

SEAL of My Own

Navy SEAL Survival
Navy SEAL Captive
Navy SEAL to Die For
Navy SEAL Six Pack

Visit the Author Profile page at Harlequin.com.

CAST OF CHARACTERS

Augustus "Gus" Walsh—Former Force Recon marine radio operator; good with weapons, electronics and technical equipment.

Jane Doe—Woman with combat training and amnesia, desperate to reach Charlie Halverson for answers.

Quincy Phishburn—CEO at Halverson International. Running the business since John Halverson's death.

Margaret Rollins—John Halverson's executive assistant, still working at Halverson International since John's murder.

Mack Balkman—Former Force Recon marine, assistant team leader and Declan's right-hand man. Grew up on a farm and knows hard work won't kill you—guns will.

Declan O'Neill—Highly trained Force Recon marine who made a decision that cost him his career in the marine corps. Dishonorably discharged from the military, he's forging his own path with the help of a wealthy benefactor.

Charlotte "Charlie" Halverson—Rich widow of a highly prominent billionaire philanthropist. Leading the fight for right by funding Declan's Defenders.

Frank "Mustang" Ford—Former Force Recon marine, point man. First into dangerous situations, making him the eyes and ears of the team.

Cole McCastlain—Former Force Recon marine assistant radio operator. Good with computers.

Jack Snow—Former Force Recon marine slack man, youngest member of the team, takes all the heavy stuff. Not afraid of hard physical work.

Chapter One

She struggled to surface from the black hole trying to suck her back down. Her head hurt and she could barely open her eyes. Every part of her body ached so badly she began to think death would be a relief. But her heart, buried behind bruised and broken ribs, beat strong, pushing blood through her veins. And with the blood, the desire to live.

Willing her eyes to open, she blinked and gazed through narrow slits at the dirty mud-and-stick wall in front of her. Why couldn't she open her eyes more? She raised her hand to her face and felt the puffy, blood-crusted skin around her eyes and mouth. When she tried to move her lips, they cracked and warm liquid oozed out onto her chin.

Her fingernails were split, some ripped down to the quick and the backs of her knuckles looked like pounded hamburger meat. Bruises, scratches and cuts covered her arms.

She felt along her torso, wincing when she

touched a bruised rib. As she shifted her search lower, her hands shook and she held her breath, feeling for bruises, wondering if she'd been assaulted in other ways. When she felt no tenderness between her legs, she let go of the breath she'd held in a rush of relief.

She pushed into a sitting position and winced at the pain knifing through her head. Running her hand over her scalp, she felt a couple of goose-egg-sized lumps. One behind her left ear, the other at the base of her skull.

A glance around the small, cell-like room gave her little information about where she was. The floor was hard-packed dirt and smelled of urine and feces. She wore a torn shirt and the dark pants women wore beneath their burkas.

Voices outside the rough wooden door made her tense and her body cringe.

She wasn't sure why she was there, but those voices inspired an automatic response of drawing deep within, preparing for additional beatings and torture.

What she had done to deserve it, she couldn't remember. Everything about her life was a gaping, useless void.

The door jerked open. A man wearing the camouflage uniform of a Syrian fighter and a black hood covering his head and face stood in the doorway with a Russian AK-47 slung over his shoulder and a steel pipe in his hand.

Her body knew that pipe. Every bruise, every broken rib screamed in pain. She bit down hard on her tongue to keep from letting those screams out. Scrambling across the floor, she moved to the farthest corner of the stinking room and crouched, ready to fight back. "What do you want?" she said, her voice husky, her throat dry.

The man shouted, but strangely, not in Syrian Arabic. He shouted in Russian. "Who are you? Why are you here? Who sent you?"

Her mind easily switched to the Russian language, though she couldn't remember how she knew it. In her gut, she knew her native language was English. Where had she learned to understand Russian? "I don't know," she responded in that language.

"Lies!" the man yelled and started toward her, brandishing the steel rod. "You will tell me who you are or die."

She bunched her legs beneath her, ready to spring.

Before he made it halfway across the room an explosion sounded so close, the ground shook, the walls swayed and dust filled the air. Another explosion, even closer, shook the building again.

The man cursed, spun and ran from the room, slamming the door shut behind him.

Her strength sapped, she slumped against the wall, willing the explosions to hit dead-on where she stood to put her out of her misery. She didn't think she would live through another beating, which was sure to come, because she didn't have the answers the man wanted. No matter how hard she tried to think, she couldn't remember anything beyond waking up in her tiny cell, lying facedown in the dirt.

Another explosion split the air. The wall beside her erupted, caving into the room. She was thrown forward, rubble falling on and around her. Dusty light spilled into the room through a huge hole in the wall.

Pushing the stones, sticks and dirt away from her body, she scrambled to her feet and edged toward the gap. The explosion had destroyed the back of the building in which she'd been incarcerated. No one moved behind it.

Climbing over the rubble, she stuck her head through the hole and looked right and left at a narrow alley down below.

At the end of the alley was a dirt street. Men, covered in dust and carrying weapons, ran along the street, yelling. Some carried others who had been injured in the explosions. The sound of gunfire echoed through the alley and the men threw themselves to the ground.

She ducked back inside the hole, afraid she'd

be hit by the bullets. But then she realized she'd rather be shot than take another beating. Instead of waiting around for her attacker to return, she pulled herself through the gap and dropped to the ground. A shout sounded on the street at the other end of the alley. She didn't wait to find out if the man was shouting at her; she turned the opposite direction and ran.

At the other end of the alley, a canvas-covered truck stood, the back overflowing with some kind of cut vegetation, dried leaves and stalks. With men shouting and brandishing weapons all around her, she wouldn't last long out in the open. She dove into the back of the truck and buried herself beneath the stems and leaves.

A metal door opened and slammed shut, the truck's engine roared to life and the vehicle rolled along the street. With no way to see where they were headed, she resigned herself to going along for the ride. Anywhere had to be better than where she'd been.

As she lay beneath the sticks and leaves, she realized they were drying stalks of marijuana, a lucrative crop for Syrian farmers. Where they were taking their crop, she didn't know. Hopefully, far enough away from the people who'd held her hostage. She touched her wrist where the skin had been rubbed raw, probably from having been tied with abrasive rope. In the meager light penetrating her hiding place, she noticed a tattoo on the underside of her wrist below the raw skin. She pushed the leaves aside to allow more light to shine in on what she recognized as a three-sided Trinity knot. Below the knot were a series of lines and shapes.

The more she tried to decipher the symbols, the more her head ached, and her eyes blurred. The tattoo wouldn't rub off. Since it was permanent, she should know what the knot and the symbols stood for. No matter how hard she tried to remember, she couldn't.

The rumble of the engine and the rocking motion of the truck lulled her into a fitful sleep, broken up by sudden jolts when the truck encountered a particularly deep pothole.

What felt like hours later, the vehicle rolled into what appeared to be the edge of a town.

If she planned on leaving the truck, she needed to do it before they stopped and found her hiding in the marijuana.

She dug her way out of the sticks and leaves, crawled to the tailgate and peered out between slitted, swollen eyelids.

The truck had slowed at an intersection in a dirty, dingy area of the town. With a dark alley to either side, this might be her only chance to get out unnoticed.

As the truck lurched forward, she rolled over the tailgate, dropped to the ground and ducked into a shadowy alley. With her face bruised and bleeding, she wouldn't get far without attracting attention. But she had to get away from the truck and figure out where to go from there.

Turning left at the end of a stucco tenement building, she crossed a street and ducked back into a residential area. Between apartment buildings, lines were hung with various items of clothing, including a black abaya cloak. Glancing left, then right, she slowed, then walked up to the clothesline, pulled off the black abaya and walked away as if she owned it.

A shout behind her made her take off running. She turned at the end of the building and shot a glance over her shoulder. An older woman stood beneath the space where the abaya had been. She wore another abaya and shook her fist.

"Sorry," she murmured, but she had to do something. With no money, no identification and a face full of bruises, she couldn't afford to be seen or stop to ask for help.

The salty scent of sea air and the cry of gulls gave her hope. If she were at a port town, she might find a way to stow away on a ship. But where should she go? She didn't know who she was, or where she belonged, but one thing she was very certain about, despite the fact she could understand Syrian Arabic and Russian, was that she was American. If she could get back to America, she'd have a better chance of reconstructing her identity, her health and her life.

Dressed in the abaya, she pulled the hood well over her head to shadow her battered face and wandered through neighborhoods and markets. Her stomach rumbled, the incessant gnawing reminding her she hadn't eaten since the last meal the guards had fed her in her little prison two days ago. Moldy flat bread and some kind of mashed chickpeas. She'd eaten what she could, not knowing when her next meal might come. She needed to keep up her strength in the event she could escape. And she had.

Walking through the thriving markets of a coastal town, everything seemed surreal after having been in a war-damaged village, trapped in a tiny cell with a dirt floor.

As she walked by a fruit stand in a market, she brushed up against the stand and slipped an orange beneath her black robe. No one noticed. She moved on. When she came to a dried-fruit-and-nuts stand, she palmed some nuts. With her meager fare in her hands, she left the market and found a quiet alley, hunkered down and ate her meal.

Her broken lips burned from the orange juice, but it slid down her throat, so refreshing and good, she didn't care. The nuts would give her the protein she needed for energy.

What she really wanted was a bath.

Drawn to the water, she walked her way through the town to the coastline, learning as she went that she was in Latakia, Syria, a thriving party town on the eastern Mediterranean Sea. People from all over Syria came to this town to escape the war-torn areas, if only for a few days.

The markets were full of fresh produce and meats, unlike some of the villages where fighting had devastated homes and businesses.

Women dressed in a variety of ways from abayas that covered everything but the eyes to miniskirts and bikinis. No one noticed her or stopped her to ask why her face was swollen and bruised. She kept her head lowered and didn't make eye contact with anyone else. When she finally made it to the coastline, she followed the beach until it ran into the shipyards where cargo was unloaded for sale in Syria and loaded for export to other countries.

By eavesdropping, she was able to ascertain which ship was headed to the US later that night. All she had to do was stow away on board. She wasn't sure how long it would take to cross the ocean, so she'd need a stash of food to see her through.

Back out to the markets, she stole a cloth bag and slowly filled it, one item at a time, with fruit, nuts and anything else she could hide beneath her abaya.

At one fruit stand, the proprietor must have seen her palm a pomegranate. He yelled at her in Arabic and grabbed her shoulder.

She side-kicked the man, sending him flying back into a display of oranges. The wooden stand collapsed beneath his weight, scattering the fruit into the walkway.

Not knowing how severe punishment was for stealing in Syria, she ran until she was far enough away, and she was certain no one followed.

With a small collection of food in her bag, she made her way back to the ship sailing later that evening to the US. Containers were being loaded by huge cranes. She found one that she was able to get inside and thought better of it. She could get in but couldn't secure the door. And if someone else secured it, she'd be locked in until the outer door was opened at the destination. Some containers weren't unloaded until they reached their final destinations…months later.

A container like that wasn't worth dying in. She'd have to find another way. The gangway onto the ship was her only other choice, and it was out in the open. She would never make it aboard in an abaya.

Waiting in the shadows of the containers she watched the men going aboard and leaving the ship. Some wore hats to shade their eyes. Others wore uniforms of the ship line or dock workers' company.

In the late afternoon, some of the men took time to eat dinner. One in particular found a shady spot to open the bag containing his meal. He sat by himself, out of view of the others in his own little patch of shade, seeming grateful for some relief from the baking afternoon sun. He wore a uniform shirt embroidered with the logo of the ship line and a hat emblazoned with the same. As he settled with his dinner, he shed his outer shirt and hat, preferring to sit in the cool spot in a tee, soaked in sweat.

Another man called out for assistance getting a container door shut.

The guy eating his dinner lumbered to his feet, leaving his shirt, hat and food in the shade. He trudged toward the other man, without looking back.

Providence.

She gave a silent prayer of thanks as she sneaked up, took the shirt, hat, chunk of bread and a plastic water bottle, disappearing before the man had a chance to return.

Though the shirt was sweaty and too big for her, it would hide any female assets and help her to look more like a man. She shoved her hair up into the baseball cap and pulled it down over her forehead enough to shadow her swollen eye.

Now, all she had to do was wait for it to get a little darker. Not too long, or they'd pull up the gangway and set sail without her. She had to get back to the US soon. If the people who'd captured her discovered where she was, she would not be safe in Syria.

Shadows lengthened with the sun angling toward the sea. The crane continued loading containers all through the day and into the evening. Men boarded and left the ship.

She waited until there was a gap in people coming and going. Pulling the cap down low over her eyes, she tucked the cloth bag full of food beneath the baggy shirt and walked across the gangway as if she belonged, hoping she appeared to be an older, slightly heavyset man getting back to work aboard the ship.

No one stopped her on the gangway.

Once aboard, she found a stairwell and descended below deck. As she went down, a man came out of a hallway several steps below.

Her heart jumped into her throat as the guy took the steps two at a time. Fortunately, he was in a hurry and ran past her without commenting. She looked away hoping he wouldn't notice she was a female with a battered face. Once she'd passed him, she let out the breath she'd been holding and hurried downward to the lowest deck she could go. Then she dodged between containers in the hull until she found a dark corner near the back. Hunkering low and pressing her body against a container, she prayed they would finish loading soon and leave port.

She must have fallen asleep while waiting. When she woke, the ship rocked gently beneath her, the rumble of an engine letting her know they were underway.

For more than a week, she rationed her food, sneaked into the galley in the middle of the night and scrounged for food and water. Like a rat lining her nest, she found a blanket and a pillow in a closet near to the crew's quarters. In the middle of the night, she used the facilities, and though she didn't feel she could linger long enough for a shower, she did manage to clean up, using a washrag and a towel.

The long journey across the water took ten long days. She filled her days trying to learn more about the ship and where it was going. Remaining undetected became a game she got very good at.

When she ventured out of her dark hole into some light, she studied the tattoo on her wrist, recognizing the squiggly lines as numbers in Hebrew. The more she contemplated them, the more her gut told her they were a set of coordinates.

When the ship finally pulled into port, she'd determined they were docking at one near Norfolk, Virginia.

As soon as she was able to sneak away, she walked into town and bought a T-shirt from a tourist vendor and jeans from a used clothing consignment store, using money she'd pilfered from workers on the ship. She ditched her uniform in a trash can and tugged on the tee and jeans in an alley. From there, she quickly found a library with computers and keyed in the numbers to find the coordinates. She learned the street address and searched county tax records to discover who lived at that street address.

A Charlotte Halverson lived there, and from the satellite street view of the location, the Halverson estate was a veritable fortress. If she wanted to get to Charlotte Halverson, she'd have to scale a wall, fight her way past security and possibly guard dogs. And for what? To tell a woman who likely didn't know her that she'd found her because of the GPS coordinates tattooed to her wrist?

A quick check on who exactly Charlotte Halverson was didn't make her feel any better about trespassing on the woman's property. She was a very wealthy widow, who employed a number of bodyguards, based on the photos of her attending various events in the DC area.

In fact, one news article reported she was scheduled to attend an upcoming charity ball at one of the swanky hotels in DC.

Getting past a stone wall and guard dogs might be extremely difficult, but she damn well could get past the security at a hotel. The event was the next night. That gave her a day and a half to get from Norfolk to DC and find her way into that hotel to get an audience with Ms. Halverson.

She prayed the woman could help her solve the mystery of just who the heck she was.

Chapter Two

"I don't need more than two bodyguards inside the hotel at the Hope for Children Gala." Charlotte Halverson, the wealthy widow of a renowned philanthropist, settled a white faux-fur shrug over her shoulders and straightened the diamond necklace around her throat. "The hotel is providing tight security. Apparently, there will be a number of celebrities in attendance for the tenth anniversary of the organization."

"What does Hope for Children do?" Augustus "Gus" Walsh asked as he fought with the bow tie that matched the tuxedoes Charlie insisted both her bodyguards wear for the event.

"They raise awareness and help combat human trafficking of children."

Gus was all for putting a stop to selling children into slavery. He'd seen too many atrocities toward children during his deployments as a Force Reconnaissance marine in the Middle East where little girls of six and seven years of age were married off to grown men.

His stomach clenched at the thought of what those little girls endured. But tonight was about glitz and glamour. Yeah, he would be completely out of his element. Give him an M4A1 rifle, camouflage paint and a mission to take out some terrorists and he would be more comfortable. Dressed in a black tuxedo that made him look like a really tall penguin with his face shaved to within an inch of his life, he wasn't feeling it. And the damned tie...

"Here, let me." The team's benefactor, Charlotte Halverson, didn't ask them to play bodyguard to her very often, but when she did, she wanted them to blend in, not stick out. Thus, the tuxedo at a black-tie event. The older woman tugged and pulled at the bow tie until she was satisfied. Then she patted his cheek with a smile. "You look magnificent." She turned her smile to the team leader, Declan O'Neill. "Both of you look wonderful. I'll be the envy of the ball. The gossiping old biddies will be jealous that I have two very handsome men escorting me." She winked. "We don't have to tell anyone that you're my bodyguards. Although, I'm sure they'll figure that out." Charlie chuckled. "I haven't gone to many galas since my husband's death, but this is one I can't miss. This organization meant a lot to John. He would want me to continue to support their efforts."

"We don't mind going. You've done so much for our group we can't begin to repay you," Declan said. He hadn't had any difficulties at all with his tie. He stood straight and tall in his tuxedo like he owned it, though it was rented.

"Oh, shush. You and your men are helping me realize a dream. One my husband had, as well. What you've done so far to help others is phenomenal. Declan's Defenders is exactly what I'd hoped for. I'm just sorry I'm using you for bodyguard duty tonight."

"Since we aren't otherwise assigned, we're glad to do it. Heck, we're glad to do it anytime." Declan lifted her hand and stood back. "You look stunning."

Charlie's cheeks reddened. "Thank you. We should get going. Arnold is chauffeuring us tonight. I don't want to keep him waiting."

Gus followed Charlie and Declan out of the widow's mansion to the waiting limousine. Mack Balkman would lead in a dark SUV and Jack Snow would follow to make sure nothing happened on their way to the Mayflower Hotel.

Charlie had already been the target of a kidnapping attempt in DC. Declan had been there when it happened and saved her from being taken. That incident had led to all six of the former Force Recon team being employed, forming Declan's Defenders.

The timing could not have been better. After being processed out of the marines with dishonorable discharges for disobeying a direct order, they'd been basically unemployable and out on the streets. Charlie had given them jobs and hope.

Gus would do anything for that woman. Including dressing up in a tuxedo to go to a black-tie gala in DC. She'd saved them all from being homeless veterans living on the streets.

Forty minutes later, after navigating traffic into the downtown district, they arrived at the Mayflower and handed off their vehicles to the valet. Gus and Declan would go inside with Charlie, while Mack, Snow and Arnold guarded the outside perimeter.

Gus counted four guards at the entrance to the hotel. A red carpet had been rolled out for the arriving guests. Ahead of them, reporters leaned over the cordon ribbon to snap pictures of a pop rock singing sensation who'd brought her latest boyfriend to the event.

Charlie waited for the young woman and her date to move on before she moved closer.

As before, the reporters leaned over the tape and snapped photos of Charlie, one of the city's leading benefactors. Gus understood that in DC,

Charlie was as much of a celebrity as the singer. She and her husband had given so much to many of the nonprofits and helped hospitals and communities with their generosity.

Gus stood beside her, trying not to blink at every camera flash, watching the crowds for anyone who might pose a threat to his boss.

Behind them, another limousine pulled up. The reporters abandoned Charlie for the latest celebrity sighting.

Finally, they were able to move into the building. Just inside the door stood two more security guards and a woman with an electronic tablet checking names against those on her list.

"Good evening, Mrs. Halverson. We're so very glad you could make it to the gala this year." The woman glanced up from her tablet and smiled. She looked from Declan to Gus. "Which one of you is Mr. O'Neill?"

Declan nodded. "I am."

"Thank you." She turned to Gus. "And you must be Mr. Walsh."

"Yes, ma'am," Gus said.

The woman chuckled. "Please, don't call me ma'am. I'm not that old."

"Yes, ma'am," Gus said again. "Miss."

She smiled again and backed up a step. "We

hope you enjoy the evening, and thank you for supporting the children who need it the most."

Mrs. Halverson swept past the woman and the guards.

Gus and Declan had to hustle to keep up with her. Once they cleared the spacious foyer, hotel staff directed them into the grand ballroom.

Already, there were hundreds of guests mingling and visiting with each other, all dressed in their finest. Men in black tuxedoes and women wearing sparkling dresses in silver, gold, blue, red and more.

The crush of people made Gus nervous. How were they supposed to keep Charlie safe when any one of the guests could easily get close enough to jab a knife into the widow?

Gus found himself stepping in front of Charlie every time someone approached.

"Gus," Charlie said. "It's okay. These people are harmless. They were all screened by the event coordinator. Now, scoot back and let me mingle with the people who paid a lot of money to support the charity. It's the least I can do to ensure this organization gets the funding needed to help the children." Charlie marched forward to a group of men and women, smiling and greeting every one of them by name.

Declan touched Gus's arm. "She should be

okay," he said, though his attention continued to be directed at Charlie and the people surrounding her.

The widow laughed at what someone in the group said. Another man with a black tuxedo and a crooked bow tie approached Charlie.

The hairs on the back of Gus's neck spiked. He started forward, expecting Declan's arm to shoot out.

His leader didn't slow him down a bit. Instead, he stepped out with Gus and swung wide around the man heading for Charlie.

Gus headed straight for the man and clamped a hand on his shoulder.

Declan stepped in front of him at the same time.

The man frowned. "Excuse me—is there something you want?"

"We're here with Mrs. Halverson," Declan said.

"Exactly who I wanted to speak with." The man looked past Declan. "If you'll excuse me, I'll just have a word with her."

Gus didn't loosen his hold on the man's shoulder. "You won't mind if we check you for weapons, will you?"

The gentleman's eyes rounded. "What?"

Gus ran his hands down the man's sides, patting his tuxedo jacket for bulges.

"I beg your pardon." The guy backed out of Gus's reach. "I do mind being treated like a criminal."

"Gus, Declan, what are you doing?" Charlie's voice sounded behind Declan.

"The man was converging on you at a high rate of speed," Gus explained. "We're making sure he isn't carrying a weapon."

"Good Lord." Charlie stepped between Gus and the man. "This is Joseph Morley, the event reporter. He always features me in his account of this gala." She turned to Joseph. "Please excuse my overzealous bodyguards. They don't know everyone."

Morley straightened his jacket and gave Charlie a tight smile. "At least they have your best interests at heart."

"Yes, they do. I can't fault them for that." She gave Declan and Gus each a narrow-eyed glare. "But they can stand back and let me have a little space while we're here."

Heat rushed into Gus's cheeks. How was he supposed to know who was friend and who was foe?

Declan and Gus took the clue and stepped back, allowing Charlie a chance to visit with Morley.

"I don't like how close everyone is to Charlie," Gus admitted.

"I know what you mean." Declan pressed his lips in a tight line. "But we can't smother her. She's already angry with us for assaulting the reporter."

"I didn't assault him," Gus said. "I only patted him down."

Declan's lips twitched. "Find anything?"

"No," Gus admitted.

"Then we should just stand back and let Charlie do her thing. As long as we keep an eye on her, she should be all right."

Gus nodded. "Sounds like a plan that will work for her."

For the next hour, they followed Charlie around the ballroom as she spoke with everyone, laughed, joked and talked about the need for funds to help keep children from being sold and trafficked in the US as well as abroad.

"Gentlemen, I shall be retiring to the ladies' room for a few minutes." She held up her hand. "I will not need your services in that area. Feel free to get a beverage and some of the appetizers. I don't plan on being here more than another hour."

Gus clamped down on his tongue to keep from saying *thank God*. He'd read that the gala started around 6:00 p.m. and didn't end until well into the wee hours of the morning.

At least Charlie didn't feel the need to dance into the night. She'd made that clear up front. They'd stay for a couple hours and then head home.

One hour down, one to go.

The patent-leather shoes he'd rented with the tuxedo were chafing at his ankles. He'd love it if he could kick off the shoes and walk barefoot through the crowd.

Gus and Declan followed Charlie through the throng of beautifully dressed people toward the hallway where the facilities were located. They gave her just enough room that she wouldn't feel crowded but stayed sufficiently close to get to her should someone try to jump her.

Out of the corner of his eye, Gus noticed a woman dressed in a long figure-hugging black gown standing near a giant potted tree. She had hair as black and silky as her dress and deep, dark eyes almost as black as her outfit. *Striking* was the word Gus would use to describe her. But what drew his attention to her was that her gaze never left Charlie. It followed her all the way into the ladies' room.

"Wanna go for that drink or appetizers while I stay and guard the door?" Declan asked.

"No," Gus said, his attention on the woman in black.

Declan must have heard something in Gus's voice. He frowned, glancing around. "Something bothering you?"

"My gut is sending up warning flags," Gus murmured.

Declan stiffened. "About?"

With barely a lift of his chin, Gus motioned toward the woman in black. "Her."

"Wow. She screams black widow in that killer

dress," Declan said. "You *are* talking about the black-haired beauty near the potted tree, right?"

"I am."

The woman looked left, then right. She spotted Declan and Gus and the slightest frown appeared and then disappeared on her brow.

"Did you see that?" Gus asked. "She frowned when she noticed us watching her."

"I thought I imagined it, but yes. I saw it." Declan turned his attention to Gus and smiled. "I'll pretend we're having a manly discussion about sports or something while you continue to watch." His grin broadened, and he spoke a little louder. "How about those Patriots?"

"You know I'm an Alabama fan," Gus said, also in a conversational volume. In a whisper, he added, "She's moving."

"Which way?" Declan asked. "Alabama is college football. The Patriots are a real team."

"Toward us," Gus muttered without moving his lips. Then he snorted. "I guess we'll have to agree to disagree."

"Yeah. You watch your team. I'll watch mine."

The woman in black sailed past them, her head held high, her silky black hair flowing around her shoulders, her chin tilted upward, displaying a long, regal neck.

Damn she was beautiful. But something about her didn't fit in with the other women in the room.

She was thin, but athletic, and she walked with confidence and purpose.

Perhaps it was the purpose that made her different than the other women in the room. Most were content to socialize and mingle. Not the woman in black. She appeared to have something on her mind and was in a hurry to get it off.

"Passing you now," Gus said, his gaze remaining on the ladies' restroom as the woman in black walked away.

"Got her in sight," Declan affirmed. "Appears to be in a hurry."

"Unlike every other woman in the room."

"Maybe she forgot to let the dog out at home."

"Yeah." Gus relaxed a little, since the woman in black appeared to be leaving and, as such, no longer seemed a threat.

Charlie emerged from the ladies' room laughing and talking to another guest similar in age to the wealthy widow. When she spotted Gus and Declan, she nodded, letting them know she was okay. Then she walked away with the other woman, rejoining the crowd in the ballroom.

Gus and Declan followed, not too far behind.

Several men came between Charlie, Gus and Declan.

Before Gus or Declan could work their way around the group of men, the woman in black appeared beside Charlie and hooked her elbow in her grip.

"She's back, and she's got Charlie," Gus said to Declan.

Gus shoved his way through the men, without excusing himself. He didn't have time for pleasantries when someone had Charlie and was leading her toward an exit door.

Caught in the group of men, Declan fell behind.

Trying not to stir up panic, Gus half walked, half ran after the two women who disappeared through the exit door into another part of the grand hotel.

His heart beating faster, Gus gave up trying to keep it cool and broke into a sprint, hitting the exit door hard, just seconds behind the two women.

The woman in black was hustling Charlie toward another door at the end of the hallway, talking in a low tone as they moved.

Charlie skipped to keep up.

Her abductor shot a glance over her shoulder, spotted Gus and glared.

"Stop!" Gus shouted.

The woman didn't follow his command, just kept moving, dragging Charlie along with her.

Unencumbered by another person, Gus caught up to the two women as they reached the exit door to the outside.

"Gus," Charlie looked over her shoulder. "I'm glad you're here."

"Let go of Mrs. Halverson," he demanded.

"Not until I have some answers," she said. "She's the only one who can help."

Gus pulled the gun from beneath his jacket and pointed it at the woman. "Let go of Mrs. Halverson."

The black-haired woman released her hold on Charlie and raised her hands. "I don't want to hurt her. I need to talk to her."

"Then set up an appointment when she's not at an event and when we can properly vet you," Gus said. "For all we know, you could be a criminal. Perhaps you should come with me and talk to the security guards. Are you even a registered guest?"

The woman's eyes widened briefly. Then as if a shutter slid down over her face, she became completely expressionless. "No."

"No, you're not a guest?"

"No, I won't go with you to the security guards." She backed up a step, then another.

"Charlie, get behind me," Gus warned.

"It's okay. She said she wouldn't hurt me."

"Please, do as I say," Gus insisted.

Charlie frowned, but moved behind him.

"Now, either you come with me willingly, or my partner and I will take you there unwillingly. Your choice."

She shook her head. "I can't." In a flash, she turned and slammed against the door, pushing it outward enough to slip through and out into the night.

Declan came running down the hallway. "Charlie, are you all right?"

"I'm fine, but I don't think that woman is." Charlie shook her head.

"Stay with Charlie," Gus said. "I'm going after her."

"I've got her," Declan said. "Go."

Gus raced through the door and out into the night. Two guards caught him before he'd gone three steps. They pulled his arms up behind him and disarmed him. "What the hell. Let me go. There's a woman I need to catch."

"She said you'd come flying out the door after her," the guard holding his right arm said.

"She also said you had a gun and you were going to kill her." The man on the left held his pistol.

"I have a conceal carry license. I'm here as bodyguard to Charlotte Halverson. That woman tried to abduct her. You should have captured her, not me."

"Right. And I'm Santa Claus." The guard on the right snickered.

Two men raced around the side of the building and ground to a stop, silhouettes in the darkness.

"Gus?" one of them said. "Did you find her?"

"Mack? Snow?" Gus called out.

"Yeah," Mack responded. "What's the problem?"

"She got away, thanks to these guards."

"Don't come any closer, or I'll shoot," said the guard holding Gus's Glock.

Mack and Snow held up their hands. "Don't shoot. We're here as bodyguards to Charlotte Halverson."

"I told them the same, but they're not buying it," Gus said. "Call Declan. Tell him to notify the man in charge of security that their guards are holding up the wrong person."

The guard holding his arm up between his shoulder blades pushed it up higher.

"Hey, you don't have to break it," Gus said. "I'm not fighting you."

Gus could hear Mack talking to Declan through his headset. A moment later, the radios clipped to the belts of the guards holding him hostage both squawked.

"Peterson, Rawlings, check the identification of the man you're holding," the voice said. "If his name is Augustus Walsh, you can release him. He's here with Charlotte Halverson and needs to get back to her."

The man holding his arm gave it one last shove up between his shoulder blades before he released it. "Sorry," he said, though he really didn't sound sorry at all. "Just doing our jobs."

"I get it," Gus said. "I was, too." He rubbed his sore arm. "If you see that woman again, detain her. She tried to take off with Mrs. Halverson."

"We will." The guard holding his weapon handed it back. "No harm, no foul."

"Yeah." Gus holstered his Glock and straightened his tuxedo jacket. "Now if you'll excuse us, we have to get back to work."

"By all means." The guard who'd jacked up his arm waved him by. "You'll have to go back around to the front of the building. The door you came through doesn't open from this side."

Gus took off, jogging. He met up with Mack and Snow.

"Did you see a black-haired woman in a long black dress?"

Mack and Snow both shook their heads.

"If you do, keep an eye on her. She tried to take off with Charlie." Gus moved past his teammates, hurrying back to the entrance of the hotel. Declan was capable of handling Charlie's safety on his own, but Gus wanted to be there in case the woman in black returned for a second attempt.

Chapter Three

She should have known Charlotte Halverson would have multiple bodyguards protecting her. A woman of her wealth and status might as well have a target on her back at all times. A person could collect a significant amount of ransom money if he successfully abducted her.

Money wasn't her goal with the Halverson woman. Answers were worth much more to her. Why did she have those coordinates on her wrist? Why did she have a Trinity-knot tattoo? Why had she been detained and tortured in Syria? Why had she been there in the first place?

More than anything...who was she?

All the effort she'd gone to in order to gain access to the gala had been a bust. All she needed was to talk to the Halverson woman and no one else. At this point, she wasn't going to risk interaction with a single soul other than Halverson. If the woman's bodyguard hadn't been so attentive she might have gotten her alone long enough to figure out the puzzle of her existence. Now she was back to square one. Not even square one. The bodyguards would think she had tried to abscond with the rich widow. They wouldn't let her anywhere near her now, and she still didn't know if she could trust anyone other than Halverson.

Once she'd made it past the guards, she'd circled the entire building, counting the number of security personnel on the outside at every entry or exit point. The only reason she'd gotten through the first time was she'd gone in as one of the housekeeping staff, with her dress and shoes tucked beneath the uniform she'd pilfered from the back of a laundry van. She'd helped clean rooms, stating she was new.

Eventually, she slipped out of sight and hid in one of the unoccupied rooms until close to time for the gala to begin. She'd showered, dressed and applied the makeup she'd borrowed from one of the rooms. The shoes had belonged to one of the guests at the hotel. Appropriately dressed, she'd found her way down a staff elevator to the kitchen and from there into the ballroom after a majority of the people had already arrived. She'd mixed and mingled as if she belonged until she'd spotted Charlotte Halverson.

Thankfully, by the time she'd made it to DC, her bruises had faded enough that makeup cov-

ered them. The swelling around her eye had all
but disappeared.

Now, standing outside the Mayflower Hotel,
frustration ate a hole in her gut. The only keys
she had to her identity were the tattoo on her wrist
and the woman inside, and she was stuck outside.
Without a coat, the cool air wrapped around her,
raising gooseflesh on her skin. She wrapped her
arms around her middle and stared at the Mayflower Hotel wishing she had one more chance.
Just one more chance was all she needed with
Charlotte Halverson.

THE WOMAN IN the black dress haunted Gus. All
the way around the massive hotel he searched the
shadows for her. Damn the security guard for stopping him from capturing her and getting answers
about why she'd tried to take Charlie.

Did she want to take Charlie away and hold
her for ransom? Had the Halversons wronged her
or someone in her family, requiring retribution?
Was there another reason she'd tried to get close to
Charlie, to give her something, tell her something?

Mostly, he couldn't forget the brown-black eyes
filled with mystery and a touch of sadness.

Who was she?

Once again, he had to run the gauntlet of the security personnel at the front door and the woman

holding the tablet with the list of names of persons who were allowed inside.

Gus wondered if the woman in black was on that list. If not, how had she managed to get past the security personnel? And if she was able to get past them, who else had done the same?

That thought made him worry that much more. Once his ID had been compared to the names on the roster, he hurried to find Declan and Charlie.

Making a beeline for the ballroom, he searched the faces, finally finding Declan, who stood with Charlie at the far end of the ballroom. Declan was easy to spot. He was a good head taller than most of the women and many of the men in attendance.

Gus worked his way around the side of the room, refusing to make eye contact with anyone, in case they waylaid him and tried to strike up a conversation. He wasn't in the mood to talk to strangers. Except maybe the woman in the black dress.

Ten minutes had passed since he'd left Charlie and Declan inside the hotel to chase after the woman who got away.

"Everything okay?" he asked when he finally reached them.

Charlie frowned. "I can't get that woman out of my mind."

Gus caught himself short of saying, *you and me both, sister.* Instead, he nodded. "Did she hurt you in any way?"

"No," Charlie said, shaking her head. "She kept saying she just needed to talk to me. Something about being the key to who she was." The older woman's frown deepened. "There was a certain desperation in her eyes. I should have gone with her."

Declan touched Charlie's arm. "We don't know who she is, or why she felt the need to drag you out of the hotel. For all we know, she could have been on a mission to kidnap you and hold you for ransom."

Charlie looked up into Gus's eyes. "I don't think so. She didn't hold a gun or knife to my head. I could have shaken free of her grip had I tried hard enough. I truly believe she only wanted to get me alone to talk to me. About what, I can't imagine. I've never seen her before in my life."

"DO YOU THINK she might claim to be a secret daughter of your late husband?" Declan asked.

Charlie snorted. "I don't think so. We didn't have children. John was infertile." Her lips curled into a sad smile. "He wanted children, but he never could have fathered them. No, the woman couldn't have been his daughter." She pinched the bridge of her nose. "I'm getting a headache. Perhaps it's time for us to leave and let the younger people stay and dance the night away." She straightened her shoulders and placed her hand on Declan's arm.

Gus fell in step at her other side.

They'd only gone a few feet when a loud, whining sound penetrated the roar of voices in the ballroom.

Gus tilted his head and listened as the noise continued. "Fire alarm."

The hotel concierge appeared at the opposite end of the ballroom, carrying a bullhorn. "Ladies and gentlemen. We're sorry to disturb your evening, but what you are hearing is the fire alarm. We need everyone to leave the building through the closest exit to you."

Declan pointed to one of the signs to the outside. "This way." He cupped Charlie's elbow and led her toward the exit. Gus cupped her other elbow and the two men escorted her out of the ballroom, into a long hallway with a bright red exit sign over the door at the end. In the hallway, the alarm was even louder.

The door at the end of the hallway, like the one he'd chased the woman in the black dress through, opened to the outside.

"Should we go out a door closer to the bulk of the crowd?" Gus suggested.

"No," Charlie said. "They wanted everyone out in case there really is a fire."

Gus pushed open the door. Before he stepped out, he looked for the security personnel first. No one stood outside. In fact, the back of the building appeared deserted.

Gus held open the door while Declan led Charlie out of the building.

"Are you guys evacuating?" Mack said into Gus's earpiece.

"We are," Declan responded. "We just stepped out of the building at the southeastern corner. We'll make our way around to the front, coming up the eastern side."

"We're on our way to rendezvous with you," Mack said.

As they rounded the corner of the building, men jumped out of the shadows and surrounded them.

Declan and Gus stepped in front of Charlie.

"We've got trouble," Gus said into his microphone.

"How much trouble?" Mack asked.

"Six deep," Gus said. Six big burly men, none of whom wore the uniforms of the paid security guards.

Gus braced himself as the men rushed them.

The first one to Gus swung a meaty fist at his head. Gus ducked and slammed his fist into the man's gut.

The man doubled over but was replaced by the next man behind him.

Gus didn't let the fact they were outnumbered

slow him down. He had to keep even one of them from getting to Charlie.

Declan had his hands full, throwing punches, ducking some and taking a couple to the jaw. The men they were fighting were trained combatants. For every punch Gus threw, they hit back with equal aim and dexterity.

While Gus and Declan fought off two each, the fifth and sixth men circled around them and grabbed Charlie's arm.

She screamed, kicked and cursed, doing her best to protect herself. But she was one woman. The two men were bigger, stronger and meaner than anything she could offer in the way of a fight.

Gus punched and kicked like a madman, but he couldn't free himself from the two men fast enough to help Charlie and neither could Declan.

Then, out of the shadows, came a whirling dervish in a black dress. She attacked the men holding Charlie, landing a side kick in one guy's kidney. She spun and swept her other foot around, hitting the other guy in the temple.

Both men staggered and loosened their holds on Charlie long enough for her to get away.

The woman in the black dress didn't stop there.

When the men reached out for Charlie again, the woman grabbed one man's arm and, using his own momentum, flipped him. He landed hard on his back, the wind knocked out of his lungs.

The other guy, seeing his partner laid low, went after the woman in the black dress. He grabbed her from behind around the middle and lifted her off the ground.

Gus had his own hands full taking care of the two who had him cornered. One pulled a knife and lunged at him. Gus grabbed the wrist of the hand holding the knife, twisted it around and slammed the knife into the second man's ribs. The man went down with the knife still stuck inside him.

An elbow to the nose of the man still standing got his attention. Gus brought up his knee at the same time he slammed the man's head down. He lay still on the pavement.

Gus went after the guy holding the woman in black.

Before he could reach him, the woman doubled over, her feet hit the ground and she flipped with the man holding her around her waist. Twisting free, she rolled out of range and came up in a ready stance.

The two men who'd fought with the woman took off, running for the shadows.

Declan's two attackers broke free, grabbed the man on the ground by the arms and hauled him to his feet. Then they ran after the others.

The man with the knife in his ribs lay groaning on the pavement, his voice trailing off as blood spilled onto the ground.

Declan ran for Charlie who stood nearby.

Gus approached the woman in the black dress.

She raised her hands. "I'm not here to hurt Mrs. Halverson. I only need to talk to her. Nothing more."

Security guards ran toward them.

"I can't stay," the strange woman said, her eyes wide as the guards came closer. "I can't let them question me."

"Meet us at the corner three blocks in that direction." Charlie pointed. "We'll pick you up in my car."

The woman hesitated.

Charlie reached out and touched her arm. "Trust me. We'll be there."

After a solemn nod to Charlie and a glance over her shoulder at the people headed toward them, the woman ran.

"What were you thinking?" Declan asked. "You don't know who she is or what she wants. She could be after the same thing those men wanted. You for ransom."

"If she hadn't shown up when she did, I might not be standing here," Charlie said. "You two were outnumbered."

Gus nodded. Charlie was right. The men they'd fought had been trained in hand-to-hand combat. They hadn't been easy to overcome. If the mystery woman hadn't come along when she had, Charlie could have been taken or killed.

"Now, let's get past all the police questions and on the road home. I want to know more about our mystery helper." Charlie started for the front of the hotel. "First off, where did she learn to fight like that? I need her to teach me a few tricks so I don't get into another situation like that. I don't like feeling helpless."

Gus would like to know more about the woman, as well. She'd impressed the hell out of him with her fighting skills. He had questions for her, too. And he wasn't so sure they could trust her. Obviously, she could take care of herself, but would she use those skills on them to overtake the team and the driver and abscond with Charlie?

THREE BLOCKS DOWN the road from the Mayflower Hotel, she waited in the shadows, watching for a limousine. Had the Halverson woman told her she'd collect her to get her to leave her alone?

Wearing only the dress and the high heels she'd worn to the party, it wasn't long before the chill night air set in. She rubbed her bare arms and stamped her feet, praying a limousine would drive up, she'd get in and the heater would be on full blast.

She'd ask all the questions after she'd thawed her cold hands and quit shaking like a blender on full speed. And she'd thought the heat intolerable in Syria.

At that moment, she could stand a good reason to sweat. If she weren't wearing the heels, she'd jog up and down the alley to get her blood moving. Alas, the straps were digging into her skin and making blisters. Running was only an option if her life depended on it.

Without a watch, she couldn't tell how much time had passed since Charlotte Halverson had promised to pick her up. Several vehicles had gone by, but none had been a limousine.

Giving up wasn't an option. She had nowhere else to go. No money, no home, no extra clothing. The jeans and T-shirt she'd arrived at the hotel in were where she'd left them when she'd changed into the staff's uniform.

She didn't think she was the kind of person who stole items on a regular basis. When she had, it had been purely a matter of desperation. Until she knew who she was, she didn't know whether she'd had a job, a bank account or a home. Surely someone missed her somewhere. Someone who knew her life history. Her name.

One thing she'd learned about herself in her journey to that corner in DC was that she knew how to fight. Her moves were instinctive. Though she'd bet they were learned. The kind of learning that required lots of practice and repetition. Training.

Had she been in the military? Perhaps she was a member of the CIA. That would explain why she had been captured and tortured. It would also explain why she had no identification papers on her.

If the Halverson woman didn't know who she was, perhaps she'd go to the CIA and ask if they were missing an agent.

Unless…she was wanted by the CIA. In which case, she would be trading one prison cell for another. And she couldn't go back into captivity. She'd die fighting before she would allow anyone to capture and torture her again.

A dark SUV slowed at the corner Charlotte Halverson had indicated. Since it wasn't a limousine, she had no intention of stepping out into the open. What if the men she'd fought with that night had come back to seek revenge on the woman who'd foiled their attempt to abduct the rich widow? She'd overpowered them once. What were the chances they'd let her get away with it again? Slim to none.

The SUV continued a little farther down the

road, inching along until it came to a full stop. A man got out and stood waiting.

Headlights indicated the approach of another vehicle.

She watched from the shadows of the alley, shivering in the cold.

Hope blossomed in her chest as a smooth black limousine pulled to a stop against the curb.

Still, she waited, not willing to expose herself to trouble when there was already one man waiting nearby. He could be there to make another attempt to nab the Halverson woman.

Another SUV pulled in behind the limousine. A second man emerged. The two men standing guard were big, muscular and held themselves with the confidence and bearing of those who'd known military service.

The limousine driver got out of the vehicle and opened the back door.

The same man who'd chased her out of the hotel in the first place emerged from the vehicle and bent to assist the rich widow out, as well. She was followed by the other bodyguard who'd been inside the hotel with her.

They stood for a moment, all looking around.

"I don't like this. You're far too exposed out here on the street," said the bodyguard who'd forced her out of the hotel.

"Gus, we promised we'd come to pick her up," Mrs. Halverson said. "I keep my promises." She turned to her other bodyguard. "Declan, have your men look for her."

The one called Declan nodded. "I will, Charlie, after you get back into the limousine with Arnold." He nodded to the driver. "If anything happens, I want you to drive. Get Charlie out of here as fast as you can."

Arnold, the driver, nodded. "I will." He held the limousine's back door open. "Mrs. Halverson, please. Let Declan's Defenders do their job. If the woman is here, they'll find her."

The widow frowned. "Fine. I'll get into the limousine…in a moment." She turned a full circle, staring into the shadows in all directions. "Young lady, don't be afraid," she called out. "I only want to thank you for helping us. Please, let me return the favor." After a long moment, she sighed and slid into the limousine.

Afraid Charlotte Halverson would leave before she told her who she was, she stepped out of the shadows into the dull yellow glow of a streetlight. "Wait. I'm here."

If it was a setup to grab her and take her to the police, so be it. With no better options and nowhere to go, she figured it was worth the risk.

Mrs. Halverson started to get back out of the

limousine. "Oh, thank God. I was worried you'd been hurt in the fight. Please, get in." The older woman changed directions and scooted across the seat, making room for her in the limousine.

The man called Gus stepped in between the Halverson woman and her. "Perhaps it would be better if she rode in one of the SUVs."

"Nonsense, Gus. She's riding with me," Charlotte said. "I'll be safe with you, Declan and Arnold to protect me." She patted the seat beside her. "Come on. Let us take you where you need to go."

"I understand your hesitation to trust me." She stared into Gus's eyes and raised her arms. "If you want to frisk me, you can. I'm not carrying any kind of concealed weapon."

Gus snorted. "You don't need to. Your hands and feet are lethal by themselves."

She held her wrists together in front of her. "If it will make you feel better, you can bind my wrists and feet to keep Mrs. Halverson safe." The thought of being held captive made her quiver inside. But she reassured herself that she could escape if she had to.

Gus glanced toward Declan. "Did you bring zip ties?"

Declan nodded. "I did." He reached into the front of the limousine and pulled out a handful of plastic zip ties.

"Oh, don't be ridiculous," Mrs. Halverson said.

"No, really. I don't mind," she said. "They are only doing their jobs and keeping you safe from me. I would expect no less." Again, she held out her wrists.

Declan slipped a zip tie around them and pulled it snug. "I'm sorry, but we don't know you, or what you want from Charlie."

Gus frowned. "Aren't you going to secure her legs?"

"Absolutely not." Mrs. Halverson glared at her bodyguards. "This woman is my guest. I won't have you treating her like a criminal. Now, let her get into the vehicle before I fire all of you."

Gus frowned heavily before he finally moved out of the way and allowed her to get in beside Mrs. Halverson.

He slid in next to her and Declan sat across from them.

"Make one wrong move," Gus said, "and I'll make sure you regret it."

The woman nodded. "I'm not here to hurt Mrs. Halverson. I only want information."

Arnold closed the back door, slid into the driver's seat and pulled in behind the lead SUV.

"Okay, now that you have my undivided attention," Mrs. Halverson said. "Who are you, and what is it you want from me?"

"That's just it," she said, her heart sinking. "I don't know who I am. I was hoping you could tell me that."

Chapter Four

Gus frowned. "Wait. What? You don't know who you are?"

The woman shook her head. "No. All I know is what I have tattooed on my wrist." She held out her hand, palm up.

Charlie gasped and grabbed her wrist. "That's the Trinity knot." She shot a glance at Declan. "What are the chances that this is a coincidence?"

"I don't believe in coincidence," Declan said, his voice tight, his jaw even tighter. "You don't know who you are? How did you know to come to Mrs. Halverson?"

The woman nodded toward the tattoo. "The co-ordinates below the symbol."

"What coordinates?" Gus stared at the tattoo. "All I see are squiggly lines."

"They're numbers in Hebrew," she said.

Gus wasn't buying her story. Who tattooed coordinates on her own body? And in Hebrew?

Highly unlikely. "How do you know they aren't a telephone number or someone's birth date?"

"I had ten days in the hull of a ship to think about it. As you can see, there are two rows of numbers. When I reached the US, I gave the telephone theory a shot. When I called the first one, it played a recording that it was out of service. I got a day care facility on the second one. Given the numbers, I figured they were longitude and latitude. The coordinates pointed to the Halverson Estate in Virginia." She stared into Charlie's eyes. "I don't have any other ideas. If you don't know who I am, I don't know where to go from here."

Charlie studied her for a long time and then shook her head. "I'm sorry, but I don't recognize you at all." Her brow furrowed. "But then I wasn't always privy to all of my late husband's activities. Perhaps he knew you?"

The woman's shoulders sagged.

Charlie reached out to her. "I'm sorry. I wish I could help you. It must be very distressful not knowing your own name. In the meantime, we have to call you something."

"Jane Doe," Gus said.

"That's so impersonal," Charlie protested.

"It's temporary until we figure out who she is," Declan said.

The woman in the black dress shrugged. "It's

as good a name as any." She nodded toward Gus. "And like he said, it's temporary. Or at least I hope it's temporary. Until I figure out who I am, I have no home, no identification and no job that I know of."

"In other words, you're broke and homeless," Gus said. "Can't blame you for chasing down a rich widow. I guess I would, too, in your circumstances."

Jane Doe's eyes narrowed. "I don't want Mrs. Halverson's money. I want to know who I am. Right now, I have no history, memories or family that I know of. If I had a job, I'm sure, by now, I've been fired for not showing up."

"You said you spent ten days in the hull of a ship," Declan's eyes narrowed. "Is that where you were when you came to or discovered you'd lost your memory?"

She shook her head, her jaw hardening. "No."

Gus leaned forward. "Where were you?"

She didn't look at him, but stared into Charlie's face. "I was locked inside a tiny cell in a small village in Syria."

Charlie's eyes widened. "Syria?"

"Yes, ma'am. Syria."

"What were you doing in Syria?" Charlie asked.

Glancing away, Jane shook her head. "I don't

know. All I know is I was held captive. That's where I woke up without my memory."

"Why were they holding you captive?" Declan asked.

"They wanted information from me." A shiver shook her slender frame. "I couldn't give them the answers they wanted."

"So, they tortured you?" Gus didn't trust the woman, but the look in her eyes was so haunting, he could almost feel her pain.

She nodded, raised both hands to touch the corner of her eye.

That's when Gus saw the faded bruise, barely visible beneath the makeup she wore. His hands clenched into fists. He didn't like seeing bruised and battered women. Men who hit them deserved to die.

"Oh, dear." Charlie touched Jane's arm. "I'm sorry you had to go through that."

"How did you escape?" Declan asked.

"There was an explosion close to the building. It blew a hole in the wall of my cell. I got out by crawling over the rubble and hiding in the back of a truck full of unprocessed marijuana."

"And the ship?" Gus prompted, amazed at the woman's tenacity and determination to be free.

"I found my way to the port town of Latakia. I didn't know where I belonged, but it wasn't Syria. Based on the language I felt most comfortable speaking and my accent, I assumed I was from the US and needed to get back there to discover who I am."

"And I failed you." Charlie sighed. "I'm so sorry."

"It's not your fault. If you don't know me, you don't know me. I'll have to keep looking until I find another clue as to my identity." Jane glanced out the windows of the limousine. "Please, let me out at the next convenience store. I won't hold you up any longer."

Silence reigned for all of three full seconds before Charlie exclaimed, "I won't hear of it. You're coming to stay with me."

Gus wanted to stop Charlie before she promised the stranger the world. But he couldn't.

Charlie was on a roll. "I have loads of room. You'll stay in one of my spare bedrooms." The older woman's eyes widened and she clapped her hands. "I'll have my men help you find the answers to your mystery." She turned to Declan. "Between you and your team and my husband's connections, we should be able to help out this poor woman."

Gus held up a hand. "Charlie, you don't know her."

"Exactly," Charlie shook her head as if speaking to a slow child. "That's why we need to help her."

"She could be a wacko out to steal from you, or

hurt you," Gus said. He glared at Jane. "We know nothing about her."

"I'm usually a good judge of character," Charlie said. "I took a chance on Declan and his recommendation for a team, based on his willingness to help me and my gut feeling that he was a good guy."

"But you knew who he was when you hired him," Gus argued.

Charlie's lips thinned. "I didn't know who he was when he pulled me out of the kidnapper's van. When I did learn who he was, I still hired him, despite the black mark on his military record."

"This is different," Gus said.

Charlie crossed her arms over her chest. "I don't think so."

"Without any identification, you can't look her up and tell if she's a convicted felon. She could have escaped from prison where she'd been serving life for murder."

"Gus has a point." Declan shrugged. "Having just escaped from prison would explain her lack of identification."

"I escaped from a prison in Syria," Jane said. "Not here in the US."

"And there's a difference?" Gus challenged.

"I was being held for the information they wanted out of me." Jane sighed heavily. "Not that it makes a difference, but they never charged me with a crime or tried me in a court. That I know of."

"The point is, my instinct is telling me to trust Jane," Charlie said. Her jaw firmed. "She's coming to stay with me. Gus, since you're so worried about her, Declan can assign you to watch out for her." Charlie smiled at Jane. "Don't let these men bother you. They're only looking out for my well-being."

"I understand," Jane said. "If I were them, I too would have great difficulty trusting a stranger. Actually, I wouldn't have let me inside the vehicle in the first place."

Gus nodded. "What she said."

"Gus, are you up for the assignment?" Declan asked. "If not, I can assign one of the other guys."

"After seeing Jane in action, I know what she's capable of." He gave the woman a narrow-eyed stare. "I'll watch her."

Jane gave as good as she got with an equally narrowed glance. "You'll be bored when you discover that I'm no threat to Mrs. Halverson."

"Charlie," the widow said with a smile. "Call me Charlie. And, Declan, please remove her restraints."

Declan frowned, but cut the zip tie binding Jane's wrists.

She rubbed at the red marks the ties had made on her skin and nodded toward Charlie. "Thank you."

"I get the feeling that being around you will be anything but boring," Gus said.

Declan chuckled. "Yes, sir. You're the right man for this job."

Gus wasn't quite certain why Declan thought it was funny that he was the right man for the job. He took protecting Charlie seriously. If that meant sticking with the black-haired beauty like a fly on flypaper then yes, he was the right man for the job.

Where Charlie's instinct was to trust Jane, Gus's was telling him where Jane went, trouble would follow.

Jane Doe.

She knew it wasn't her name, but it gave her hope that it was only temporary.

When they arrived at the entrance to the Halverson estate, Jane studied the impressive stone fence and wrought iron gate. Yes, she was almost certain she could have gotten in, but she didn't know what kind of security system the Halversons had in place. She might only have gone two steps before a guard dog ripped her to shreds or a dozen heavily muscled men converged on her, aiming automatic rifles and fully loaded handguns.

Invading a person's private residence might not have gotten her invited in like meeting the wealthy widow at a gala. Not that her execution had gone exactly according to her original plan. In the long run, she was here, going in under the watchful eye of her assigned guard.

Charlie had no idea who Jane was, but her promise to help her find answers was better than being turned back out on the streets where she'd had to steal to survive.

"I don't like taking charity," Jane said. And she didn't like stealing. "If there is something I can do to repay you, I'm more than happy to earn my way until I'm able to return home." Assuming she had a home. Hell, for all she knew, she might live in Syria, not the US.

Deep inside, she didn't think so. But her memory only went back as far as the beatings she'd endured at the hands of her captors. Anything before that was a complete blank. Why she knew how to speak Russian and Arabic was just as much a mystery to her as her fighting skills.

The caravan of vehicles drove on the curving road through an archway of ancient oaks. When they emerged from the wooded acres, Jane's breath caught in her throat at the three-story mansion ahead. They pulled into a circular drive and stopped at a marble staircase leading up to a massive double door.

A woman and two men emerged and came down the steps.

Arnold, the driver, parked the limousine and

hurried around to open the door. Gus got out and offered his hand to Jane.

She felt certain she wasn't used to having a man help her out of a vehicle. Given the dress and high heels, she accepted the hand.

He pulled her to her feet with enough force she bumped against him.

Jane planted her hands on his rock-hard chest and looked up into his deep brown eyes, reflecting the light from the front entrance.

"I'm watching you," he whispered and then held her until she was steady on her feet before stepping back to offer his hand to Charlie.

He was gentle helping the older woman out of the vehicle.

Jane had the urge to plant her foot in his backside. She resisted, knowing it would only buy her a little satisfaction for a short time and make her look bad to her benefactor. Until she got the answers she needed, she had to play nice with the cranky guard assigned to look after her.

"Charlie, are you all right?" The woman who'd exited the house hurried forward to engulf Charlie in a hug.

"Grace, of course, I am." Charlie glanced around at the other men exiting the SUVs. "I take it good news travels fast?"

"Mack called ahead and let me know what happened," Grace said. "I knew I should have gone with you to the gala."

Charlie shook her head. "I'm fine. I had sufficient backup and a little help from my new friend Jane." She turned to Jane. "Jane Doe, this is my personal assistant Grace Lawrence. Grace, this is Jane. At least until we figure out who she really is."

Grace shook Jane's hand. As soon as she released it, she frowned, her gaze shooting to Declan. "I don't understand."

"I'll explain later," he said. "Right now, let's go inside. We didn't get a chance to eat at the gala and I'm hungry enough to eat a side of beef."

Grace stepped back, allowing Charlie to move ahead.

Charlie led the way into the house, not stopping until she arrived in a large, modern kitchen. "Carl," she called out, looking around.

A barrel-chested man wearing a white chef's smock and carrying a canister emerged from what appeared to be a walk-in pantry. "Yes, ma'am."

"We have a lot of hungry people converging on your kitchen," Charlie said. "What have you got?"

Carl grinned. "I'm about to pull a ham out of the oven. I'd planned on having ham and eggs for breakfast tomorrow, but we can eat it now. I can steam some vegetables in just a few minutes and toast some baguettes."

"Perfect. What about wine?"

"I'll get the wine," Grace offered and headed for a door on the far end of the kitchen.

"I'll help." Declan followed. They descended a staircase that led downward, possibly into a wine cellar.

Carl grabbed mitts and turned to one of the two ovens. When he pulled the door open, steam rushed out along with the heavenly scent of baked ham.

Jane's knees wobbled and her stomach gave a loud rumble. How long had it been since she'd eaten a good meal? She'd scrounged for everything she'd eaten over the past two weeks since her escape from her cell in Syria. While held captive, her meals had been few and inadequate. She'd probably lost ten or fifteen pounds she couldn't afford to lose.

While the men shrugged out of their jackets, Carl set the ham on the counter and carved off a stack of slices. "If you're too hungry to wait for vegetables, you can make sandwiches." He pulled out a loaf of fresh bread and sliced the entire thing, laying it on a plate beside the ham.

"That's what I'm talking about," one of the men said.

Charlie laughed. "Don't worry about the steamed vegetables. Lettuce and tomatoes will suffice. I think we're all ready to eat now, not twenty minutes from now."

"Done." Carl hurried to the refrigerator, extracted the requisite lettuce, tomatoes and condiments and returned to the island. In less than a minute he had everything sliced and ready.

Grace and Declan emerged from the wine cellar, carrying two bottles each of red wine. Gus reached into a cabinet and retrieved wine glasses, handing several to Jane before loading his hands with more. They carried them to a huge table in the corner of the kitchen.

Carl made sandwiches to order one by one, starting with Charlie. Once they had their plates, the men and women moved to the table and claimed seats. Carl brought his own plate and several bags of potato chips and joined them.

Once everyone had a chance to eat several bites, Charlie went around the table, introducing everyone.

She nodded toward the brown-haired, blue-eyed man who'd ridden along with them in the limousine. "You met Declan O'Neill at the gala. He's the leader of my team of former Force Recon marines."

Declan gave her a chin lift.

Charlie nodded to Gus who'd taken the seat next to Jane. "And you met Augustus Walsh who has been assigned to protect you."

Jane almost snorted, but held back. Protect her? The hell he was. He was going to keep an eye on her to keep her from hurting Charlie or any of his band of brothers. Jane nodded politely. "Do I call you Augustus?"

"Just Gus," he said in more of a grunt than polite conversation.

Her lips twitched. "Okay, Just Gus."

His glare was worth the teasing, making Jane's smile broaden.

"Next to Gus is Mack Balkman," Charlie continued. "He was at the Mayflower Hotel tonight pulling outside guard duty."

A man with black hair and blue eyes lifted a hand. "We got caught up in the evacuation of the ballroom and missed the fight."

"Jack Snow was outside the hotel as well," Charlie said.

A tall man with dark blond hair and gray eyes winked. "Declan says you held your own with two attackers." He nodded. "I'm impressed."

Jane shrugged. "I did what I had to."

"For which I'm extremely grateful," Charlie said. "You met Grace." She nodded to her assistant and then tipped her head toward a man with brown hair and brown eyes. "Frank Ford was security backup here at the estate, along with Cole McCastlain who works with my computer tech Jonah Spradlin, who isn't here tonight."

The man she'd called Frank Ford gave a chin lift. "You can call me Mustang."

The man with the close-cropped hair and hazel eyes Charlie had introduced as Cole nodded.

"Do you have a different name you go by?" Jane asked.

"Cole is it," he answered.

"Gentlemen and Grace," Charlie announced, "this is, for all intents and purposes, Jane Doe. Our mission is to discover who she is and help her find her way home."

Home. The word filled Jane with warmth and hope. She prayed she had such a place and that a family was there to welcome her.

Chapter Five

"You don't know who you are?" Mack asked.

Jane shook her head. These former military men had every right to be suspicious of a woman claiming she didn't know her own identity.

"How did you end up with Charlie?" Grace asked.

Jane showed them the tattoo on her arm and explained about the numbers in Hebrew. She ended her life history with, "Now you know as much as I do."

"I'm amazed you knew how to read Hebrew," Grace said.

"I've discovered I can understand and speak Russian and Arabic and that I know how to fight."

"I'm even more impressed," Grace said. "My friend Emily is a Russian instructor and translator. It's not an easy language to learn. And I can imagine Arabic is even harder."

"The question is why she had the longitude and

latitude of the Halverson estate tattooed on her wrist," Declan said.

"All I can think is that it might have had something to do with my late husband's secret activities." Charlie lifted her glass of wine and sipped. "It might be worth a trip to his corporate office to see if he left any files. As for that matter, we can tear apart his home office and see if we can find anything that will help. It's about time I figured out what he was up to. He kept secrets from me, telling me it was better that I not know some of the things he was doing. He assured me it was all for the good. The good of what, I don't know. But I trusted him. John was a good man. He only wanted to help people."

"Mack and I can go through the home office tomorrow," Declan said. "I can have Cole go through your husband's computer."

Charlie frowned. "Jonah already has, and he couldn't find anything."

"A second set of eyes might help," Declan said.

"I'll work with Jonah and see if we can find anything," Cole said.

"Would it help if I went to your husband's office?" Jane asked. "Maybe somebody there will recognize me."

Charlie tilted her head, as if considering Jane's request. "That's not a bad idea. With nothing else to go on, it won't hurt to try."

"Then Jane and I'll go tomorrow," Gus said.

"I'll go with them," Jack Snow added.

"And I will, too," Charlie said. "You'll need my permission to get in."

"Thank you all," Jane said. "I don't know what else to do. For now, I'm completely at your mercy."

Grace ran an assessing gaze from Jane's head to her toes. "I think between Charlie and I, we can come up with some clothes for you to wear until we can get you to a store."

"If I can get back to the Mayflower, I left some jeans and a T-shirt in one of the broom closets."

"I'm sure by now, they have been discovered and tossed." Charlie patted Jane's shoulder. "We'll take care of you."

"As long as I can repay you when I can," Jane insisted.

"Sweetheart," Charlie said, "as far as I'm concerned, I should repay you. Between you, Declan and Gus, you saved me from those men tonight."

Heat rose up Jane's neck into her cheeks. "You don't owe me anything. I would have done that for anyone under attack."

"But it was me, and I'm thankful. The least you could do is let me help you."

Though she wanted to refuse, Jane couldn't. The truth was she needed Charlie's help. "Okay, but any clothes you purchase, I'm keeping receipts. I'll pay you back as soon as I can."

"Deal." Charlie smiled. "Now, if you'll excuse me, it's way past my bedtime. Good night, all."

As soon as she left the kitchen, the others came to the same conclusion.

"Cole and I are headed out," Mack said. "We shared a ride earlier."

"I'll be back early tomorrow morning to start sifting through Mr. Halverson's computer files," Cole said. "We'll see if we can find information about his secret operations and our mystery lady, Jane."

"I'm out of here," Jack said. "Let me know when you leave the estate. I'll meet you at the Halverson corporate offices."

"What do you want me to do?" Mustang asked.

"You can ride along with us and help protect Charlie," Gus said.

"Then I'll be back bright and early." Mustang gave a mock salute and headed for the door.

"I moved the vehicles around to the side of the house," Arnold said.

"Do you have any clothes with you, Gus?" Grace asked.

"Fortunately, I brought something to put on besides this rented tuxedo. I didn't want to wear this penguin suit any longer than I had to. I also have a bag with my workout clothes in it."

"Good," Grace said. "As Jane's bodyguard, you'll be here for the night."

By the look on Gus's face, he'd already made up his mind to stay wherever Jane would be.

Jane shivered at the intensity of his determination to protect Charlie and his team from her. She admired that in the man. He was loyal and true to his friends.

"Jane, if you'll come with me, I'll show you to your room," Grace said.

"If Charlie has a suite, that would be ideal," Gus said. "Since I'm staying with Jane."

A shiver of awareness rippled across Jane's skin. She raised her eyebrows, pretending a cool reserve she wasn't feeling. "Is that necessary?"

"Absolutely." Gus crossed his arms over his chest. "I can't keep an eye on you if you're in another room."

She lifted her chin. "You're not sleeping with me." Her belly tightened. Holy hell. What would it be like to sleep with this man whose broad chest and thickly muscled arms could sweep any woman off her feet? Even one as tough as she.

"Not to worry. I have just the suite you'll need." Grace led the way up a sweeping, curved staircase to the third floor. "Charlie keeps these rooms for special guests."

"Ones who can climb all these stairs, I hope," Gus said.

"Of course." Grace chuckled. "You and Jane will have the Rumba Suite."

Grace opened the door. Inside was a large sitting area at the center and two bedrooms, one on either side of the sitting room.

"Will this do?" Grace asked.

"Yes," Gus said.

"No," Jane said. "I'm not comfortable having a strange man in my bedroom."

"Oh, he won't be in your bedroom," Grace said. "You'll have one of the bedrooms, and Gus will have the other. You'll have to share a bathroom and a sitting area. I think this will work out just fine."

Jane wasn't so sure. Considering her situation, and the fact she had no home, no money and no identity, though, she could deal with sharing a suite.

"It'll work," Gus said.

Apparently, whether she liked it or not, they were going to share the space.

After a glance around the posh interior, Jane couldn't complain. It beat the hell out of the filthy dirt floor of the cell she'd been confined to in Syria.

Jane eyed her guard. If the man tried anything, she had the fighting skills to defend herself. What she couldn't understand was why she'd ended up locked in a cell, if she could fight like she had outside the Mayflower hotel? Then again, she'd been weak from hunger and beaten pretty badly. For a moment, she closed her eyes and tried to remember anything past the day she'd woken up in that cell. No matter how hard she tried, she couldn't drag even a shred of a memory from the depths of her mind.

"Jane? Are you okay?" Grace asked.

Jane opened her eyes and gave a weak smile. "I'm fine."

"I'll be back in a few minutes with clothing you can use until we can get you to a store."

"Thank you." Jane walked around the sitting room and into the bedroom on the right.

Gus did the same, entering the bedroom on the left. He walked out of that room and passed her as she emerged into the sitting room.

"Was the other room not satisfactory?" she asked, standing in the room's doorway.

He entered the bedchamber on the right and walked across to the window. After opening the window and poking his head out, he closed it again. He came to a stop in front of her. "This room will do for you. The other has a trellis up to the window."

"Why is that important?" Jane asked.

"It could either be a good way to escape or be attacked. Take your pick. I prefer to be the one manning that room with that drawback."

"Are you afraid I will attempt an escape?" She snorted. "Where would I go? I have no money, no family that I know of and no job—again, that I know of."

"You could be lying and setting us up to slit our throats in our sleep."

"Or I could be telling the truth." Jane heaved a heavy sigh. "Look, I don't expect you to trust me. I'll have to earn your trust, if I want it."

He nodded. "That sums it up."

"I found some jeans and a top that might fit you, and a nightgown." Grace's voice sounded from the door to the suite.

Jane spun to face her, heat climbing her neck into her cheeks. "Okay. Thank you."

Grace's eyes widened as she stared from Jane to Gus. "Did I interrupt something?"

Gus pushed past Jane. "Not at all. While you sort through clothes, I'll go grab my stuff from my truck." He paused on his way out, a frown furrowing his brow. "That is, if you're okay being alone with her."

Grace smiled. "I'm sure I'll be just fine. It will give us a chance to do some girl talk."

Gus shot a glance at Jane, his eyes narrowing. "I'll have Declan come check on you."

"No need," Grace assured him.

Jane bet her life Gus would have Declan come up anyway.

He left the room, albeit reluctantly.

"I trust my instincts. And my instincts say you

won't hurt me." Grace handed Jane the stack of clothing she'd brought with her. "The jeans might be a little big on you. You're so thin, compared to me."

That's what happens when you don't get nourishing meals on a regular basis, Jane thought, but didn't voice. "I'm sure they'll be fine. Anything, at this point, is better than nothing."

"I also provided a bra and some panties. Everything is fresh and clean. We can shop tomorrow for things that will fit you better." Grace tipped her head toward the bathroom. "There's plenty of shampoo, conditioner and body wash in the cabinets in the bathroom. If you need anything else, just let me or Arnold know. We probably have some of just about everything in the storeroom." She stood for a moment, her arms empty, her brow dipping. "It must be frightening not to know who you are."

Jane wouldn't say frightening. Waiting for the next beating in a dirty cell in Syria was what nightmares were made of. "More frustrating than frightening," she admitted.

"If anyone can help you, it's Charlie and Declan's Defenders." She smiled a friendly smile. "They helped me when my roommate went missing. And they helped my roommate through some troubling times. Trust them—they'll do everything in their power to get you the answers you so desperately need."

"Thank you," Jane said. Grace seemed like a really nice person. Genuinely caring and trusting of these people who'd taken Jane in despite her questionable background. "And thank you for the clothes."

Declan showed up in the doorway, a smile on his face.

Just as Jane expected. A smile curled her lips. Gus was predictable if nothing else.

"Are you finding everything you need?" he asked.

"Yes, thanks to Grace," Jane said.

"Don't worry," Declan said. "We're going to get to the bottom of our mystery guest."

"I hope you don't regret what you find," Jane said. She really did like these people. What if they learned she was some kind of criminal with a checkered past? Or worse, a serial killer? Her breath caught in her throat and lodged there. What if she was a terrible person? Maybe she couldn't remember because she didn't like who she was. What if the men who'd beaten her did so because she'd deserved it?

GUS HAD HURRIED DOWNSTAIRS, found Declan and asked for someone to keep an eye on Jane while he gathered his things. Declan hadn't hesitated, climbing the stairs two at a time to the third floor.

With Declan as backup, Gus hastened out to his truck, grabbed his gym bag and the clothes he'd brought to change into after the gala. The sooner he got out of the tuxedo, the better he'd feel. He hoped he hadn't damaged the suit in the fight outside the Mayflower. The tuxedo rental company would probably charge full price to replace it.

He had no doubt Charlie would reimburse the cost, but she already did so much for him and the rest of the team.

Gus made his way back up the staircase to the third floor, feeling a sense of urgency to get back to the job of watching Jane.

When he arrived at the suite he'd share with her, he found Grace and Declan standing in the doorway.

"I'm sure whatever we find will be good. You seem too nice to be anything but good," Grace assured the woman.

"Everyone who knew Ted Bundy thought he was a charming, nice man," Gus said. "Except the girls he murdered."

Grace gasped. "Gus, surely you don't think Jane is another Ted Bundy."

Jane's gaze met his, her face devoid of expression, but her dark eyes widened slightly, as if in fear. That look lasted a split second and then was gone.

What was she afraid of? That he was too close to the truth, and too close to revealing the criminal she was? He couldn't help but feel that she feared the truth about herself.

Was the woman who could take on two men at a time in a street fight really vulnerable? Was she being honest? Had she lost her memory?

Gus shook away the thought. He couldn't let himself go soft on Jane. Until he knew everything there was to know about her, he couldn't let his guard down for a minute. Too many of the people he cared about most could be at risk with her living amongst them. Charlie's generosity toward a stranger could get them all in trouble.

Declan clapped a hand on Gus's shoulder. "Holler if you need anything. We're only a floor away." He took Grace's hand in his.

"That goes for you, too, Jane," Grace said. "Have a good night's sleep."

Finally left alone, Gus tipped his head toward the bathroom. "You can go first in the shower."

"Thanks," she said. "I don't think I normally wear high heels. If I ever wear them again, it'll be too soon." She gathered the pile of clothing Grace had brought and carried all of it into the bathroom, closing the door behind her.

Once alone in the suite, Gus did another pass

through. Though there were two bedrooms, Gus wouldn't be sleeping in his. He wouldn't hear her movements. She could sneak out of the suite in the middle of the night without him knowing.

He tested the couch in the sitting room. It was firm, but manageable. Though a little short for his tall frame. It would have to do. He'd hang his feet over the edge if he had to.

While the shower was going, he pulled the comforter off the bed in his room and carried it and a pillow to the couch. The sitting room had a set of French doors leading out onto a small balcony. It was high enough up, it would be a stretch to think someone could jump to the ground and not end up with a broken neck. Still, if Jane decided to leave that way, she'd have to pass him on the couch. He'd have to sleep with one eye open.

He walked to the suite door and studied it. How would he keep her in the room? The couch was close enough he would know if she tried to go through the French doors. Being on the third floor, he was almost certain she wouldn't attempt the drop.

At the very least, he needed a way to rig the door to make a noise if she tried to leave.

"Why don't you just move the couch in front of the door and sleep there?"

Gus turned to find Jane standing in the doorway

of the bathroom, a terrycloth robe cinched around her narrow waist.

"What if you try to go out the French doors?" he asked.

"Then I deserve the broken neck I would get from that foolish a move." She carried the stack of clothing Grace had brought, the black dress folded neatly on top, the high-heeled shoes dangling from her fingertips.

Barefoot and makeup-free, her wet black hair slicked back from her forehead, she appeared to be not much older than a teenager. And the bruise around her eye was more pronounced.

Gus's chest tightened. He knew how cruel some men in Arab countries could be toward women. Hell, toward anyone. If what she said was true and she'd escaped a place where she'd been beaten, she was a brave woman with a whole lot of gumption.

He wanted to admire her, but he couldn't let himself. Not until they knew more about her. Mostly, he wanted to rip apart the men who'd beaten her.

Jane entered the bedroom and placed the clothing on top of the dresser.

She turned back to him. "Come on. You won't get any rest if you're worried about me taking off." Jane crossed the sitting room to the couch. She gave it a good shove, but it didn't move. "It's heavier than it looks."

Gus joined her at the other end and leaned all of his weight into it while she pulled it toward the door. It moved, but only a few inches at a time.

She gave him a crooked smile. "At least you'll know I won't be able to move it, if you're not helping me." Jane dug her bare feet into the carpet and leaned back, pulling at the arm.

Little by little, they shoved the couch toward the door.

"We can stop short of the door. As long as it's close, I'll hear if anyone tries to get in or out. I don't want to create a fire hazard by blocking our only safe exit."

"Nice of you to think of me." Her lips twisted. "But for now, go ahead and move it up against the door."

"Why?"

Jane propped her fists on her hips. "If you want to get a shower, you won't feel comfortable leaving me alone in here by myself."

She was right. He wanted that shower after wrestling with the attackers at the hotel. He leaned into the couch and, with Jane's help, shoved it against the door.

"And you can leave the door to the bathroom open. I'll even sit on the couch so you can keep an eye on me." Jane raised both hands, palms up. "See? I'm trying to make it easy for you."

His eyes narrowed.

Jane rolled her eyes. "I know. You still don't trust me any further than you can throw me."

His lips twitched. "I could probably throw you pretty far. You don't look like you weigh very much."

"You don't get much to eat when you're held captive by Syrians who don't like you very much." The words came out like a statement of fact. She didn't appear to be fishing for pity.

Still, his gut clenched. Jane was too thin. She could use a hamburger a day for the next month to put some meat back on her bones.

Gus rummaged in his gym bag for shorts, ready to get the hell out of the fancy clothes and into something less constricting. He glanced at Jane.

Jane held up a hand. "I do so solemnly swear to be right here when you get out of your shower." Then she sat on the couch, tucking her legs beneath her.

She'd been beautiful in the figure-hugging black dress, but seeing her in the white robe, her dark hair a stark contrast to the white terrycloth, she took his breath away.

Whoa, dude, he counseled himself. He couldn't get all wrapped up in this woman. Even if she awakened in him a desire he hadn't felt toward a woman in a long time.

He hurried into the bathroom and closed the door just enough to allow him to strip with a little privacy, but open enough he could look out and check to see she was as she said she'd be…on the couch.

Once naked, he peered around the edge of the door.

Jane smiled and waved. "Still here."

Gus stepped in the shower, turning on the water to a lukewarm setting. He was far too aware of his nakedness with a half-open door the only thing standing between him and the woman who'd taken on two attackers without breaking a fingernail. She wasn't wearing much beneath the robe and she had long, sexy legs that seemed to go on forever, disappearing beneath the robe's hem.

Once beneath the spray, he turned the water cooler, hoping to chill the rise of heat in his loins.

Jane was the job. Nothing else.

Hell, her name wasn't even Jane. What was it? He focused on a name that suited her to keep from thinking about those long, bare legs.

Salina? No. Jezebel? Maybe. She talked all innocent, but he suspected she had a fire burning deep inside. He could imagine how passionate she'd be in bed. A fierce fighter, she had to be no less fierce in bed.

And there he was back to thinking about her in a purely unprofessional manner. He turned the water cooler. By now it was so cold, gooseflesh rose on his skin.

In quick, efficient movements, he washed his hair and body and switched off the cold water. When he reached for the towel, he realized he'd forgotten to get one out of the cabinet.

A hand reached around the curtain extending a towel toward him. "Take it," Jane's voice said from the other side.

He snatched the towel from her and held it low in front of him. "What the hell are you doing in here?"

She stood on the other side of the opaque white curtain, her body silhouetted in hazy gray. "Getting a towel for you. When I got into the shower, I forgot a towel and had to get out to get one. I figured you might have done the same. I was right?"

"Yes," he said, hating to admit it. "But I could have gotten it myself."

"With the door open?" She snorted softly. "I figured you were a little more modest than some."

He wrapped the towel around his waist, praying he wouldn't make a tent out of it. Then he flung the curtain aside. "Thank you."

She stepped back, her gaze running the length of him from head to toe. "Glad I could help." Her lips curled and she pointed at his torso, just about his belly button. "You missed a spot." Then she turned and left the bathroom and Gus, getting aroused to the point his towel tented.

Sweet hell, the woman was going to make him

crazy. Thankfully, she'd sleep in the bedroom. The couch would be sufficiently uncomfortable to take his mind off the woman in the other room.

He closed the door just enough she couldn't see him. Gus slipped into the shorts and opened the door again.

Jane wasn't on the couch where she'd been when he'd gotten into the shower.

Gus's heartbeat galloped ahead. The couch was still in front of the door where he'd left it and the French doors were closed.

"I'm in the bedroom, in case you're wondering," Jane called out.

The breath he hadn't realized he'd been holding whooshed out of his lungs and he remembered to draw in a fresh one.

She leaned out the door, her smile twisted. "You thought I'd left, didn't you?"

By not answering, he gave her his answer.

Jane shook her head. "I told you, I don't have anywhere else to go. I'm homeless and I can't even get a job because I don't have an identity. No social security number, no driver's license and no car. How am I supposed to live?"

"You made it this far in two weeks from Syria?"

She pressed a hand to her flat belly. "Hungry, stealing to survive and hitchhiking on a container ship isn't my idea of a good time. If the authorities randomly stop me, I'll go straight to jail.

They might even deport me, claiming I'm an illegal alien. Hell, I might be." She sighed heavily. "So, you see, I'm staying here until I figure out who the hell I am. I won't hurt Charlie or anyone working for her. Why would I bite the hand that's feeding me?"

Gus held up his hands. "Okay. I'll give you the benefit of a doubt for now. But I'm still sleeping on the couch."

Jane shrugged. "It's your back. I can't tell you the last time I slept in a real bed." She yawned, pressing a hand over her mouth. "I'm looking forward to clean sheets and a comforter to keep me warm. You do what you have to. I'm going to bed." She turned away, slipped the robe from her shoulders and laid it on the end of the bed.

The nightgown she wore was icy blue and barely covered her bottom. She pulled back the comforter and sheet and slipped into the bed. "Good night, Gus. I really do hope you sleep well. I plan on it." Then she pulled the comforter up to her neck and reached over to turn off the light.

For a long moment, Gus stared at the darkened room.

"Go to sleep, Gus," she called out softly.

Gus moved the couch a little away from the door, enough they could get out if needed, but not enough Jane could slip by without him noticing.

Then he stretched out on the comforter, his gaze on the bedroom door.

He lay awake for a long time, a dozen questions racing through his mind, all centering on the woman in the other room. Frustrated that he didn't have any more answers than he did, he could only imagine how Jane felt, not knowing who she was.

If she really didn't know.

Chapter Six

When Jane lay on the soft bed, in the clean sheets, with her head snuggled against a feather pillow, she fell asleep as soon as she closed her eyes, thinking heaven couldn't be more comfortable.

How long she slept, she couldn't tell. But the heaven she'd fallen asleep in soon turned to hell. She was back in the cell in Syria, waiting for the next visit from the men who'd beaten her.

The smell of urine burned her nostrils and the cold hard ground pressed into her bones. She'd lost track of how many days she'd been there and couldn't remember how she'd gotten there in the first place. Her captors kept asking her questions she couldn't answer. They asked the same questions and she gave them the same answers. She couldn't remember. No matter how many times they hit her, she still couldn't tell them what they wanted to know.

She lay on the dirt, dried blood crusting on

her lip and nose, her eye nearly swollen shut, and prayed for a miracle.

The door opened and a man yelled at her to get up.

When she couldn't, he stalked into her cell and kicked her hard in the ribs.

She cried out, loud enough to wake herself out of her dream.

Still shaking, her rib still hurting from the dream kick, she sat up in the nice, soft bed and wrapped her arms around her legs. Going back to sleep was not an option. If she did, she'd be right back in that cell, suffering from the latest abuse.

She tried to think about anything other than Syria and the stench of her cell.

Jane. They call me Jane Doe. Whispering softly to herself, she tried to talk herself down from the nightmare. "You're not in Syria. You're in Virginia. You're not being beaten. You're okay." Her eyelids drifted downward. Once…twice…

As soon as they closed, she was right back in that cell, her captor yelling down at her. Again, she opened her eyes, forcing herself back to consciousness.

When she thought she might fall asleep again, she pushed aside the comforter and left the bed, padding barefoot to the open door.

In the pale light from the stars outside the window, she could see Gus lying on the couch, his arms crossed behind his head, his eyes closed.

She wanted to wake him to talk to her and ground her in Virginia. But he looked so peaceful and asleep.

Jane sat on the carpet in front of the French door, determined to sit up all night. If she didn't go to sleep, she couldn't dream. If she didn't dream, she wouldn't end up back in Syria, wishing she could just die and get it over with.

Through the window, the stars shone, filling the sky like so many diamonds brilliantly sparkling. When she'd been in her cell, she hadn't had a window to see outside. She'd gone days without fresh air or sunshine. Days passed, but she didn't know how many or how long she'd been in her cell.

Now, sitting on a comfortable carpet, she should be grateful and happy that she was clean, well-fed and pain-free. But she couldn't relax, couldn't settle until she knew.

Who was she? Why had they captured her? What had they wanted from her?

Sitting in a plush house with all the food she could possibly eat, an endless amount of hot water for showers and people who could help her, she felt anxious, restless and worried.

If she could, she'd do her own sleuthing. By herself. That way if she learned anything about herself that was unfortunate or heinous, only she would know. She could live with that. But if Charlie and her team of former military men, Declan's Defenders, learned that Jane Doe was a horrible person, she would feel that she'd let them down. All of their help would have been for naught. She'd have to leave, if they didn't turn her over to the police, FBI or CIA first. A shiver rippled through her, shaking her entire body. She couldn't bear to see the hate and disappointment in their faces after all they'd already done for her. And Gus would have been right to be suspicious.

She looked back at the couch and her heart stood still.

Gus was gone.

Jane sat up straight, her body tense, her pulse now pounding, shooting adrenaline through her system.

"I didn't mean to sneak up on you." Gus appeared from behind her, carrying the blanket from her bed. "I thought you could use this." He draped it over her shoulders. "I would have said something, but you were pretty caught up in whatever you were thinking about."

Jane wrapped the blanket around her shoulders and pulled it close. "Thank you."

"Couldn't sleep?"

"Didn't want to," she replied.

He went back to the couch, grabbed the comforter and returned, spreading it out on the floor beside her. "Bad dreams?"

She pulled her knees up under her chin and wrapped her arms around her legs. "Yes."

"Sometimes it helps to talk about them." He lifted a shoulder and let it fall. "Or so my shrink said. I don't always buy into that crap."

She laughed softly. "In this case, I don't think talking about it would help. It would only reinforce the memory."

"Oh, so you have one?" He turned toward her, his eyes wide, questioning.

"Only from my captivity. And those are memories I'd rather forget."

"Right." He looked out the window. "If it helps, I thought some of my worst memories would never fade. I had nightmares for years about a mission gone incredibly bad. But the memories finally faded. They aren't gone, but their impact doesn't plague me nearly as much as it did in the beginning."

Jane crossed her arms over her knees and rested her chin on them. "I don't even have any good memories to think about to counteract the effects of the bad ones." She wasn't whining, only stating the facts. She didn't want pity from the man beside her. Only understanding.

"Yeah. That's gotta be tough."

She looked at him, her eyebrows raised. "So, you believe me about my memory loss?"

He gave a twisted smile, still staring out at the stars. "No, but I can imagine what it would be like not to remember the good times in life."

"What are some of your good memories?" Jane asked. "Maybe I can borrow yours to think about when I'm in a bad place."

He continued to stare out the window without speaking.

After a long moment, Jane didn't think he would respond.

"The day I left the foster care system and joined the military is one of my best memories."

"You were a foster child?"

He nodded. "Since I was seven and my parents and little sister died in a car crash on their way to pick me up from school. That was one of the days I had nightmares about for years," he said, his voice so low, she barely caught his words.

"I'm sorry. It must have been hard for you."

He shrugged. "You learn to keep moving. If you sit too long, you get swallowed by sadness. I kept moving. I got shuffled from one foster family to another. The first family had a boy of their own about my age. He was a bully and made my life pretty miserable. I put up with it until one day he shoved me so hard, I hit my head on the concrete sidewalk. I came up dizzy but fighting mad, and bloodied his nose."

"The beast deserved it," Jane said, wishing she could have been there for the little boy who had it hard enough dealing with the deaths of his parents.

"The boy's parents blamed it all on me. I got placed with another family who had two other foster children. One was a teen with drug issues. The other was his brother, a kid just trying to survive in a world that had let him down. The teen ended up overdosing on meth. The foster parents were so distraught they quit the program and the two of us were farmed out to other homes. I had six different foster homes before I graduated high school. And I only graduated high school because I knew that's what my mother and father would have wanted. I joined the marines to get away from it all."

"I'm sorry you had to go through all that."

"I'm not. You don't know the good times unless you had the bad times to compare it with. I'd forgotten what it felt like to have a family who cared. Until I signed up for Force Reconnaissance."

"Your team is your family?"

He nodded. "I'd give my life for any one of them. And they'd do the same."

Jane sighed. "You're lucky."

"Who knows?" Gus said. "We might find out that you have a whole family waiting to hear from you."

"Or not. I feel like, deep in my gut, there isn't anyone out there waiting for me." She stared out the windows of the French door.

"Don't give up yet," Gus said. "Cole is pretty good at anything internet related."

Jane gave a weak smile. "How can anyone find information about a person who has no basis or starting point?"

"The FBI and CIA do it all the time. Charlie has contacts in both from dealings her husband had with them. We'll find out who you are soon enough."

"And if you don't like what you find?"

"We'll cross that bridge when we come to it."

Jane yawned and laid her cheek on her folded arms. "I'm so tired."

"Would it help if you leaned on me? Maybe having someone close will keep you from reliving your nightmare."

"Why would you do that?" She stared at him, her brow furrowing. "You don't even trust me."

"You know the saying… Keep your friends close but your enemies closer?" He gave her a crooked grin.

"Some say Sun Tzu was the originator of the quote," Jane said. "But he said something like, 'know your enemy and know yourself and you will always be victorious.'"

"So, you've studied Sun Tzu?"

Her frown deepened and she stared at the ground. "I must have."

"Perhaps some of your memory is starting to come back."

"I hope so," she said.

"In the meantime, the offer still stands. You're welcome to lean on me."

She sighed. "I'm willing to try anything for a chance at dream-free sleep."

Gus scooted closer and held open his arm. "Come here."

She leaned into him and snuggled her cheek against his chest. "At least you won't have to worry about me sneaking out while you sleep," she said, her eyes drifting closed. Fully expecting the nightmares to continue, she waited.

Nothing. No images of angry men slapping her around, punching her and kicking her in the side. Just the arousing scent of male cologne and the reassuring feel of rock-hard muscles beneath her cheek. Gus, his military fighting skills and the backing of his band of brothers in arms would ward off the men who wished to hurt her in her dreams.

Jane drifted into a deep sleep. Her only dreams consisted of a man who held her gently, surrounding her with a feeling of family she was sure she'd never known.

GUS HELD JANE the rest of the night. At one point, he eased her down onto the comforter beside him and pulled her back against his front, spooning her body.

He told himself he only did it because it made it easier for him to keep track of her. If he were honest, he would admit he liked having her close.

Seeing her sitting on the floor in the borrowed nightgown, her long black hair hanging down her back and her narrow shoulders hunched, touched him somewhere he hated to admit existed. Because if it existed, it left him vulnerable in a way he hadn't been vulnerable since his parents had died.

In some ways, she reminded him of the little boy he'd been with his trash bag full of whatever he could carry from his home to his foster family. He'd arrived at a strange house where nobody knew him and they knew each other. Every house he had gone to, he'd been the outsider, the person who didn't really belong.

He saw that in Jane and it made his chest hurt.

Granted, she wasn't a grieving seven-year-old who'd lost her parents. But, if she was telling the truth, she had lost a lot more than her family. She'd lost the memories that made her who she was.

Gus had faded memories of the father and mother who'd loved him, and the little sister who'd idolized him from the time she could talk. He had those memories to pull out whenever he was in a bad place.

What did Jane have? Memories of being beaten and held in a dirty cell in Syria?

His arm tightened around her, pulling her closer. He rested his cheek against her silky black hair and inhaled the scent of her skin. The first time he'd seen her he'd been impressed with her beauty. The long, sleek lines and raven-black hair had captured his attention, even before he realized she'd been watching Charlie's movements.

From the strength of her determination to get to Charlie and the answers she so desperately desired, to the vulnerability of a woman fighting horrific nightmares, she made Gus think. About her, about her story and about his own reaction to the way she felt in his arms.

The situation had *bad idea* written all over it.

Yet Gus couldn't let go. She felt right in his arms. Her body fit perfectly against his. She wasn't too tall or too short. Jane was just right.

Gus must have fallen asleep.

Sunlight filtered through his closed eyelids, forcing him to crack them open. He lay for a moment in the sunlight, letting the bright rays warm his body.

Jane lay with her head on his biceps and one leg slung across his thighs, making it impossible to rise without waking her. Her breathing was deep and steady. No signs of despair or nightmares.

Though he ached from lying against the hard floor, Gus couldn't regret having defended the woman against her bad dreams. Not when her warmth pressed up against him with only the thin fabric of her nightgown between them.

As he lay there, desire built from a spark to a flame. The longer he held her the more he wanted. She was not someone he could make love to. She was an assignment, the job, his responsibility, not his lover.

Gus had to get up and move away.

He slipped his legs from beneath hers and was in the process of scooting his arm from beneath her head when she blinked her eyes open.

She stared into his face, a slight pucker forming on her forehead. "Who…what…" Then as if recognition dawned, she bolted to an upright sitting position. "I must have fallen asleep." She pushed the hair from her face and turned toward the sun shining through the window. Her eyes widened. "It's morning."

Gus chuckled and sat up, pulling the comforter across his lap to hide the evidence of his desire. "Yes, you slept and it's morning."

She shook her head. "I'm sorry I took advantage of you. It couldn't have been comfortable sleeping on the floor."

"I've slept on worse."

For a long moment, she stared out the window, the pulse at the base of her throat pounding hard. Finally, it slowed and she turned back to him. "Thank you. I don't think I've slept that well in… well, I don't really know how long."

With her hair mussed and her face pink from sleep, she was even more beautiful than she'd been in the black dress the night before. Despite the faint bruise near her eye. The soft morning sunlight added a certain vulnerability, making her no less mysterious, but more approachable.

The more he stared, the more he realized he was getting caught in something he wasn't ready to deal with.

Gus pushed to his feet, immediately turning away from Jane. "People are usually up pretty early around here. Carl will have breakfast ready before we get downstairs. You should probably get dressed." And he should take another cold shower. But he couldn't explain the need without revealing why. Instead, he grabbed his jeans and held them in front of himself, waiting to dress until Jane went to her bedroom.

"I won't be long," she said.

The sound of the door closing behind him gave Gus the chance to release the breath he'd been holding. He quickly slipped into his jeans and eased the zipper up over the hard ridge of his erection. He pulled on a T-shirt and let it hang loose over his waistband, hoping to hide the evidence long enough for his desire to abate.

Socks and shoes came next and then he shoved the couch back to where it belonged in the sitting room. He collected the comforters from the floor and draped them across the couch.

The bedroom door opened and Jane stood framed in the doorway, wearing dark slacks, a soft pink sweater and black shoes. She'd brushed her hair back from her face and tucked it behind her ears.

She lifted her chin and gave him a tight smile. "I'm ready when you are." The vulnerable woman of minutes before was safely hidden behind a poker face.

Gus couldn't imagine what this woman had gone through and was currently going through. His gut was telling him to trust that she was telling the truth. But what if she wasn't? He worried that his desire made him soft and vowed to remain vigilant to protect his team and Charlie. "I'm ready." He was ready to bring on the day and all that it might reveal.

Chapter Seven

Jane must have imagined the gentleness in the way Gus had held her the night before. His look as he opened the door to the suite had shifted back to the professional military man on a mission. She couldn't blame him. He had a job to do. Knowing how he felt about his team, she would expect no less. They were his family and he had to protect them at all costs. From her.

Her chest tightened as all the horrible scenarios she'd come up with the day before resurfaced. Today could be the day that they learned who she was. Originally, she'd thought knowing was better than not knowing. Now she wondered.

Though he was all professional and cool, Gus held out a hand to her at the top of the staircase.

She laid her fingers in his palm.

He closed his hand around hers. Without a word, he started down the staircase to the ground floor.

They followed the voices coming from the

kitchen. Before they reached it, Jane pulled her hand free of his. If she turned out to be a threat to his team, he didn't need to explain why he'd been holding the hand of the enemy.

Some of the team were already there. Jane went through the names she remembered. Cole, Declan, Arnold, Carl, Grace and Charlie were gathered, along with a man she didn't recognize.

"Oh good," Charlie turned to smile at them. "I was about to send Grace up to check on you two. Carl has breakfast ready. I trust you slept well?"

Jane nodded. "I did." She couldn't vouch for Gus, since he'd slept on the floor with her in his arms. This, she didn't share with her benefactor. In this case, less information was better.

"Cole and Jonah have been up and working the computer since six this morning." Declan nodded toward a man Jane hadn't met. "Jonah, Jane. Jane, Jonah Spradlin, Charlie's tech guy."

A younger man with blond hair and gray eyes nodded in her direction. "Hey."

"Nice to meet you." Jane's pulse quickened as she faced Cole and Jonah. "And? Did you find anything?"

Cole shook his head. "We've used all the passwords Jonah knew when he worked with Mr. Halverson, but haven't cracked the secret databases yet."

"We're working on it," Jonah said, "but it might

take a little more time to hack in. He had it locked down pretty tight."

Jane didn't know whether to be frustrated or glad that they didn't know anything yet. She leaned toward frustrated. If the news was bad, she'd deal with it. Who she was in the past didn't set the course for who she could be in the future. Unless she ended up in jail. Jail put a damper on planning for a future. Still, she couldn't borrow trouble. She'd cross whatever bridge she came to, when she reached it.

Mustang arrived as they gathered around the table.

"Where's Snow and Mack?" Mustang asked as he set a plate on the table, pulled up a chair and sat.

"They're going to meet with one of my CIA contacts at Langley," Charlie said as she scooped scrambled eggs onto her plate. "They're going to check into Syria and see if they can find a connection to a woman fitting Jane's description."

"Do you happen to recall the name of the town you were held captive in?"

Jane shook her head. "I have no idea. I was too worried about getting out of it to stop and ask."

Charlie gave her a gentle smile. "Not to worry. They'll get whatever intel they can and bring it back here for us to sift through."

Jane found it difficult to breathe. Her chest was so tight, air didn't seem to want to move in or out. She stared down at the food on her plate for a long moment, vivid images of her cell, the explosion, the rubble and the back of the truck carrying marijuana all flashing through her mind at once. How long would it take for them to fade into dull memories?

A large hand settled on her left knee and squeezed.

She looked up into Gus's face, glad he was next to her. His strength and determination gave her hope for a future of her own choosing. If a seven-year-old boy could overcome a difficult upbringing, Jane would work through her flashbacks until they no longer consumed her.

Forcing a deep breath into her lungs, she resumed regular breathing and attacked the meal in front of her. If her situation got bad, she might be back out on the street. She'd need her strength to keep going.

"Charlie." Jane set her fork beside her plate, having eaten every last bite. "Do you mind if I ask, what happened to your husband?"

Charlie shook her head. "I don't mind your asking." She took a deep breath and let it out before answering. "He was murdered."

Jane's heart contracted. She'd known he was deceased, but murdered? "I'm so sorry. Did they get who did it?"

Charlie's eyes narrowed. "No. There was no

evidence to go on. He was shot leaving his office building. There were no witnesses and the security cameras showed nothing. The police suspect a highly trained sniper pulled the trigger. I hired a private investigator to look for the man who killed John. We found nothing."

"So, the murderer is still running free."

Charlie nodded. "When someone tried to kidnap me, I was fortunate enough that Declan was nearby and saved me from my kidnappers. That's when I decided to employ Declan and his team of marines. Too much gets by the police. I wanted a way to help others so they didn't have to go through what I've endured."

"We're lucky to be here." Declan tipped his head toward Charlie.

"I'm lucky to have you and your team on my side." Her brow wrinkled. "Something that keeps surfacing in the situations we've encountered are references to Trinity." She tipped her head toward Jane. "Like the symbol on your wrist. We've seen it now several times. We aren't sure what it has to do with what's happening and why all these events seem to tie together."

Declan shook his head. "That's something I asked Mack and Snow to check into while they're visiting your contact at the CIA. Maybe they can come up with the connection or an explanation of what the Trinity symbol stands for in this situation."

Jane rubbed the tattoo on her wrist. It had been the only thing she'd had to go on when searching for her identity.

"I've been thinking we should bring Cole or Jonah with us to my husband's office," Charlie said. "If we need to get onto his desktop computer, we'll need someone who knows his way around."

"I can continue to work on getting into John's computer here at the house," Jonah said. "If I find anything, I'll notify you immediately."

"Thank you." Charlie's gaze swept the room. "I can be ready in ten minutes."

"I'll pull the vehicles around to the front," Arnold said.

Charlie turned and left the room.

"Ten minutes," Declan said. He and Grace rose and started to gather plates from the table.

"Don't worry about the dishes." Carl waved them away. "I'll take care of them. You have more important things to do."

"Thanks, Carl," Declan said. "And thanks for breakfast. You always feed us well."

"Yes. Thanks, Carl," Jane said. "The meals are truly delicious."

Carl beamed. "I do my best. Can't ask for a better job."

Jane almost envied the chef. To know who he was and enjoy the job he performed had to be satisfying. What kind of job had she had before she lost her memory? What kinds of jobs took a woman to Syria? She spoke a few languages and she had fighting skills. Could she be a member of the CIA? Maybe she should be going to Langley with Mack and Snow. But if she were a double agent, working for the Russians or Syrian rebels, going to Langley could get her in hot water.

Letting Mack and Snow take on that task seemed to be the right answer for Jane. She didn't want to end up being interrogated by the US government any more than she had been interrogated by her Russian captors in a Syrian village.

She glanced toward Gus. He might be her guard to protect his team and Charlie from anything she might throw their way, but he'd actually become her protector, as well. She found comfort knowing he was there, and he was strong and a capable fighter. If she were attacked, he would help her to escape. At least, she hoped he would.

Just as Charlie had said, they met ten minutes later in front of the mansion where three vehicles were lined up. Instead of the limousine, Arnold would be driving a luxurious town car.

"Grace and I will ride with Charlie and Arnold," Declan said. "Cole will take the lead SUV and Gus will follow in the SUV with Jane."

They climbed into their assigned vehicles and the convoy drove out of the Halverson estate and into DC.

"Does Charlie always have lead and trailing vehicles when she goes places?" Jane asked.

"She's been attacked twice since we've known her," Gus said. "It makes sense to provide her with as much security as we can."

"She's a generous woman." Jane frowned. "Why would anyone want to hurt her?"

"Her husband was equally generous from all accounts I've heard. Why would someone want to kill him?"

"Charlie said he had secret activities he was involved in. Perhaps that was what got him killed."

Gus nodded. "That's our bet. I hope we learn what those activities were sooner than later. I have a feeling they are the reason someone has tried to take Charlie twice now."

"They might think she knows more than she does."

"Could be. Let's hope Cole is more successful getting into her husband's computer at his office than he's been on John's home desktop."

Jane sat in the passenger seat, staring at the car ahead of them carrying the woman who'd opened her home to a stranger who could prove to be a danger to her. Charlie might have put her trust in the wrong person when she invited Jane into her home.

Jane clenched her hands into fists. No matter who she had been in her past, she refused to harm one hair on Charlie's head in the future. The woman had a heart of gold. She treated the people around her like family. Anyone would be lucky to be a part of Charlotte Halverson's family.

THEY ARRIVED AT Halverson International Headquarters in downtown DC. The five-story Georgian-style white building with its tall columns and huge entry doors stood on a corner and stretched for an entire block.

Gus was thankful they had no more problems than the usual stop-and-go traffic getting into downtown DC. No one tried to run them off the road or hijack Charlie's car. When they arrived, they drove right into the reserved parking lot beneath the Halverson building.

Charlie led the way inside.

Security guards snapped to attention and ushered her and her entourage through to the information desk where her guests were given lanyards with temporary passes attached. One by one they scanned their passes through the turnstiles and were finally through to the interior.

Charlie used her ID card inside the elevator, taking them to the top floor.

When she stepped out of the elevator, a mature woman in a gray skirt suit, with faded red hair combed into a neat French twist, met her there.

"Mrs. Halverson. It's so nice to see you. Can I get you and your guests something to drink?"

Charlie turned to the group who'd followed her into her husband's office. "This is Margaret Rollins. If you want to know where anything is, ask her. She was my husband's assistant. She knows as much, if not more, than my husband did about this business."

Margaret nodded. "Thank you."

Charlie gave her a brief smile. "I'll be conducting a meeting with my guests in my husband's office. I'd appreciate it if we were not disturbed."

"Of course, Mrs. Halverson. Please, come this way." The woman led the way down a long hallway to a massive wooden door at the end. She pushed through into a spacious office suite with a reception desk guarding another office behind it.

"Would you prefer to be in Mr. Halverson's conference room, or his office?" Margaret asked.

"His office, please," Charlie said. "If I recall, he had sufficient seating for all of us."

"Yes, ma'am. Nothing's changed since…" She stumbled on her words for a moment and then seemed to get a grip. "Since your husband's passing."

Charlie touched the woman's arm. "That's nice to hear."

"It's really good to see you here," Margaret added.

"I should have come sooner. It's just hard to

come here and not see John sitting at his desk." Charlie gave her husband's executive assistant a weak smile.

"I understand," Margaret said. "I had a hard time coming back to work knowing he wouldn't be here." She sighed. "I'm thinking about retiring at the end of the month. But I'm glad I got to see you again before I leave."

Charlie took the woman's hands in hers. "I'll be sorry to see you go. I know I should have stepped in sooner to take over. I just couldn't. But I'm here now."

"I'm glad you are. You and Mr. Halverson will always have a place in my heart. You've been so good to me."

"He couldn't have done the job without you, Margaret." Charlie looked past her to her husband's office and her bottom lip trembled.

Margaret squeezed her hands. "Go on in. It's just as he left it."

Gus could see Charlie's hesitancy. Except for a few brief meetings in the office building, she never went there. He sensed it was too painful.

Grace hooked Charlie's elbow on one side and Declan on the other.

Charlie shot them a grateful smile, took a deep breath and moved forward into the office where her husband had successfully led his company for more than three decades.

Gus, Jane and Cole followed, giving the widow a little distance to come to grips again with her loss.

John Halverson's office took up the entire corner of the building, with floor-to-ceiling windows overlooking downtown DC and many historic buildings and landmarks. He even had a shiny brass telescope positioned to overlook the Washington Monument.

Charlie walked to his desk in the center of the room. It appeared to be only a desk without a computer or monitor.

Gus looked around for the computer. Had someone taken the desktop computer out of his office when he'd passed? The secretary had indicated his office was just as he'd left it.

Charlie gave a small smile. "He was so proud of the work he'd done, building his business in international trade to what it is today. I never begrudged him the time he spent late into the evenings working so hard. Often I'd bring dinner to him and we'd have a picnic here in his office with the night skyline shining through the windows."

No one said a word, allowing Charlie to remember the good times she shared with her husband.

She drew in a deep breath and pressed her finger into the desk. A computer monitor popped up from a panel in the surface.

Charlie looked up at Cole. "You'll want to sit at his desk to access his computer." She laid a slip of paper beside the monitor. "These are the passwords he used when he was alive. I don't know if they've been reset."

Cole grinned and hurried forward. "I was beginning to wonder where it was hiding." He sat in the leather executive office chair and pulled it forward. Within seconds, he had the computer booted and was keying away, using the passwords provided.

Charlie walked to a credenza against the far wall and pressed her thumb against a fingerprint scanner and a door slid open exposing a file cabinet. "We can go through these paper files while Cole looks through the digital ones." She moved over several feet to another fingerprint scanner and pressed her thumb there. Another door opened to reveal yet another file cabinet. "My husband kept a lot of records over the years. Before he died, he must have known he might meet an early demise. He had me come in one evening and gave me access to the files only he had access to. He had my thumbprint and my eye scanned. And he gave me a list of his passwords, telling me not to share them with anyone I didn't trust completely." She shot Cole a glance. "I trust Declan's Defenders with my life. I guess that's as completely as you can get. Until now, I didn't see a need for you to go through my husband's information."

Cole nodded. "Your secrets are safe with me, Charlie."

"And me," Declan echoed.

"As well as with me," Gus said.

"And me," Grace added.

Which left Jane. She held up her hand. "Charlie, I know it's too early for you to put full trust in me, but I swear on my life, your secrets are safe with me, too."

Charlie smiled. "Thank you."

They went to work going through every file in every cabinet, spreading them out on the small conference table in one corner of John's office. After an hour, a voice sounded over the phone intercom.

"Mrs. Halverson, Quincy Phishburn, the acting CEO, would like to have a word with you."

"Could you schedule him for an hour from now?" Charlie asked.

"He said he only has a small window of opportunity to meet with you between other meetings. He'd like to see you now."

Charlie glanced around at the file folders spread out over the conference table. "Where?"

"In John's office," Margaret said.

Charlie pressed a button on the phone. "I have it on mute."

"We can set things to rights in under a minute," Grace said. She nodded to Declan, who grabbed up a stack of files and carried them to the cabinet. Grace, Gus and Jane carried the files they'd been working through and placed them in the cabinets. Moments later, the cabinet doors were closed.

While they had restored the files to their proper places, Cole shut down the computer and the monitor disappeared into the slot on the desk.

Charlie looked around at the neat room and pressed a button on the phone. "Please, show Mr. Phishburn in, Margaret."

Cole joined Gus, Jane, Grace and Declan at the small conference table as the door opened and a man with graying temples, wearing a charcoal-gray pinstripe suit, entered the office and crossed the room quickly toward Charlie.

Gus, Cole and Declan were halfway out of their seats to intervene when Charlie raised a hand and gave a little shake of her head.

Phishburn took Charlie's hands in his. "Mrs. Halverson. What a pleasure it is to see you here."

She smiled at the man. "Thank you, Quincy. It's been too long."

"We understand. Losing a loved one is never easy." He released her hands and turned to the people gathered around the table and frowned. "I trust everything is all right?"

"Quite," Charlie said. "I'm only here because I

needed a place to meet with my team on a project I'm working on."

"And what project is that?"

"Nothing that concerns the corporation," Charlie said. "And I'll be coming to the office more frequently. So, you can expect to see me more often."

Quincy's attention jumped back to Charlie. "Are you concerned about the corporation or my performance?"

"Not at all. I'm an owner in this business and I need to be as involved as my husband was."

"Mrs. Halverson, there's no need for you to feel as if you have to fill your husband's shoes. He hired a team of employees to run the business. We're all quite capable."

Gus's fists clenched at the patronizing tone in Quincy's voice. The man didn't understand Charlie at all.

He didn't have to worry about the widow. She was more than capable of defending herself. "Quincy, dear, I'm quite certain you are capable, but the corporation needs owner oversight to make certain it's headed in the intended direction." She tipped her head up, looking down her nose at the man. "I'll be in next week to start reviewing profit-and-loss reports, balance sheets, sales and marketing. Of course, I will take all the advice I can get, but I'm aware of how this organization runs, having worked with my husband more years than you've been with Halverson International." She walked toward the door and opened it. "Now, if you'll excuse us, we have work to do."

Gus swallowed hard to keep from laughing out loud.

"Yes, ma'am." Firmly put in his place and his cheeks a ruddy red, Quincy Phishburn left the office.

Charlie closed the door with a loud click and shook her head. "I really despise men who think they know more than me just because I'm a woman. I earned a bachelor's degree in international marketing at Harvard and my masters in operations management at Yale. I'm not an idiot." She went to the cabinets again and opened them with her thumbprint. "Let's get this done. Obviously, I need to come here more often. And I will."

Cole leaped to his feet and got to work pulling up the computer and digging into the files.

An hour later, they admitted defeat.

"I'm not finding anything on this computer, or in any of the corporate databases," Cole said. "I dug into Phishburn's files and noticed he has a Fantasy Football spreadsheet with tabs dating back several years."

"I don't care about his football bets," Charlie said. "But I will be checking into the job he's doing for the corporation. I might be making some management changes in the near future. Although, John hired him, so he must have seen something in his credentials." She snorted. "I threw my degrees at him, but they don't mean squat if you don't have the intelligence to find your way out of a paper bag."

"Charlie, we all know you've got paper bag navigation down pat," Grace said, with a smile tugging at the corners of her lips.

"It's a good thing you're pretty," Charlie said with a stern look. Then a smile broke free. "Most important, you have a big heart and a sense of humor. Those are key in my books." Charlie clapped her hands. "Let's head back to the house."

"I'd like to make a stop along the way, if we can," Gus said.

"Where?" Charlie asked.

"At a marine recruiter's office I know of." Gus locked gazes with Jane. "They have a fingerprint kit I'd like to borrow."

Declan grinned. "Good idea. They keep more than criminals' prints in the system."

"Perfect," Charlie agreed. "I hadn't thought about that, but Jonah has a friend in the FBI with access to the IAFIS system. For that matter, he might have direct access, via hacking. He can run

Jane's prints. She might show up in the government employee or military database."

Jane grimaced and added softly, "Or the criminal database."

Chapter Eight

"Are you okay with that?" Gus asked.

She nodded. "I need to know who I am. No matter the outcome."

Gus's thoughts had run along the same lines, but it could be one of the fastest ways to get to the bottom of who Jane Doe really was.

Charlie touched her arm. "Don't worry. I don't think you're a criminal."

"But what if I turn up on that database as having committed a crime?"

"We'll worry about that *if* it happens. And I'm betting it won't." Charlie gave her a quick hug. "Come on—we might find out who you are sooner than we thought."

They left John Halverson's office.

Charlie stopped at Margaret's desk. "Have a nameplate made up to replace John's. I'm moving into the office next week."

Margaret smiled. "Thank God. I might even put off retirement, if you plan on staying a while."

"If you want to retire, go ahead. But I'd really like it if you stayed." She gave Margaret a hug.

"Mr. Phishburn won't be happy that you're going to take over where Mr. Halverson left off."

Charlie winked. "All the more reason for me to step in."

Margaret grinned and sat behind her desk. "I'll have that nameplate up before the end of this week."

Charlie led the way out of the suite to the elevator. "I've let grief keep me on the sidelines far too long. I have too many good years left in me before I sell the business." She stepped into the elevator, her lips firm, her head held high. "John would want me to do this."

"You're a smart woman," Grace said. "You'll do great things."

"You know that means you'll be coming to the office with me every day."

Grace smiled. "I know. I'm okay with that."

"We'll have to dedicate a space for Declan's Defenders."

Gus could almost see the wheels turning in Charlie's head.

"We're flexible," Declan said. "We don't need a dedicated space."

"You might not, but I do," Charlie argued. "I

like having a war room to plan and strategize. There's a conference room next to my office. It will serve nicely as a war room for you."

"Like I said," Declan repeated, "we're flexible."

"Then it's settled," Charlie stood straighter. "I'll have Margaret get corporate badges for you to enable you to get in and out of the building easily."

Declan gave her a mock salute. "Yes, ma'am."

They left through the garage and pulled out onto the street, Gus and Jane in the lead vehicle, Cole in the trailing SUV.

Gus led the convoy to the marine recruiting headquarters. A man he'd gone through marine basic training with had landed there as a recruiter. They agreed that only Jane and Gus would go into the office. The others would wait out in the parking lot in their vehicles.

Gus led the way into the office. Jane followed.

"Can I help you?" A young lance corporal manned the front desk.

"I'm looking for Staff Sergeant Haines."

"One moment, sir." The corporal punched a button on the desk phone in front of him. "Sergeant Haines, you have guests in the front office." He released the button and looked up. "He'll be right with you."

A black man wearing the Marine Corps dress blues walked out of a back office, grinning. "Walsh, you old son of a gun. What brings you

FREE BOOKS GIVEAWAY

GET TWO FREE BOOKS & TWO FREE GIFTS WORTH OVER $20!

We pay for everything!

YOU pick your books –
WE pay for everything.
You get TWO New Books and
TWO Mystery Gifts...absolutely FRE

Dear Reader,

I am writing to announce the launch of a huge **FREE BOOK GIVEAWAY**... and to let you know that YOU are entitled to choose TWO fantastic books that WE pay for.

In return, we ask just one favor: Would you please participate in our brief Reader Survey? We'd love t hear from you.

This FREE BOOK GIVEAWAY means that we pay for *everything!* We'll even cover the shipping, and no purchase is necessary, now or later. So please return your survey today. You'll get **Two Free Book** and **Two Mystery Gifts** altogether worth over **$20!**

Sincerely,

Pam Powers

Pam Powers
for Reader Service

Complete the survey below and return it today to receive 2 FREE BOOKS and FREE GIFTS guaranteed!

FREE BOOKS GIVEAWAY
Reader Survey

1

Do you prefer stories with suspenseful storylines?

◯   ◯
YES   **NO**

2

Do you share your favorite books with friends?

◯   ◯
YES   **NO**

3

Do you often choose to read instead of watching TV?

◯   ◯
YES   **NO**

YES! Please send me my Free Rewards, **2 Free Books** and **Free Mystery Gifts**. I understand that I am under no obligation to buy anything, as explained on the back of this card.

❏ I prefer the regular-print edition
182/382 HDL GNVY

❏ I prefer the larger-print edition
199/399 HDL GNVY

FIRST NAME	LAST NAME

ADDRESS

APT.#	CITY

STATE/PROV.	ZIP/POSTAL CODE

to a recruiting office? Don't tell me you want to sign up again?"

Apparently, word hadn't gotten out about Gus's dishonorable discharge from the Marine Corps. Otherwise, Haines wouldn't have suggested signing up again, as that wasn't a possibility. Gus preferred to keep it that way.

"I need a favor," Gus said.

"Name it. I owe you a few from basic. I don't think I'd have made it through without help from my old pal Walsh." He held out his hand.

Gus took it and was pulled into a bear hug that took his breath away. "Good to see you, Haines."

"You too, man." He clapped him on the back and stood back. "Now, what's this favor you need?"

"Do recruiting offices still have fingerprint kits?"

"I think we might have one around here somewhere. We rarely throw anything away. Come on back to my office. I have a supply cabinet back there. If I have one, it'll be there."

Gus stepped aside to allow Jane to pass.

"Who've you got here?" Haines grinned. "A recruit for us?"

"Not this time." He turned to her. "This is Jane Dole," he said, obviously forgoing the Doe surname so as not to trigger questions. "She's a new recruit to the company I've gone to work for. We need to run a background check on her."

"You know they have companies that do that kind of thing for you."

"I know, but my boss didn't want to spend the money." Gus hated lying to his friend, but the truth would take a lot longer to explain. "I was hoping to get the prints and have a buddy of mine run the check."

"Gotcha." Haines opened a metal cabinet full of office supplies and military gear. He dug around inside and came out with an ink pad and a couple blank fingerprint cards. "You know how to do this?"

Gus nodded. "I think we've got this."

"I'll give you a hand, just in case." Haines set out the ink pad and the card.

One by one, he rolled Jane's fingers in the ink and then into the corresponding block on the card.

When they were done, he showed her to the bathroom where she could wash up.

"It's good to see you," Haines said. "I'd heard you'd gotten out." He shook his head.

Gus stiffened. Just what had he heard?

"Whatever the charges were, I'm betting it was all bullshit," Haines said. "You were always straight up and gave one-hundred-percent. Not everyone makes it into Force Recon. I always knew you could. I have the utmost respect for you, man." He held out his hand. "Semper Fi."

Gus gripped the man's hand, his chest tight. "Semper Fi. Thanks." For helping him with the fingerprinting and for believing in him when the powers that be in the Marine Corps hadn't.

Jane joined him and they left with the card. Minutes later they were on the beltway, headed back to the Halverson estate. Gus and Jane took the trailing vehicle position.

"What was Haines talking about, charges?" Jane asked.

"I left the Marine Corps with a dishonorable discharge," he said, his tone flat, discouraging further conversation.

"I'm sorry to hear that," she said. "What happened?"

"We made a command decision to disobey an order that would have had extreme consequences and collateral damage." Gus snorted. "Because of our decision, our team took the hit and we were shown the door."

Jane stared across the console at Gus. "I'm betting you and your team did the right thing. Politics can be harsh, even when you do the right thing."

He shot a glance her way. "And you know that because?"

She stared out the windshield at the vehicle ahead. "I don't know why I know that. I just do."

"It doesn't take a genius to figure it out, either,

but then the higher ranks and politicians aren't always geniuses. But thank you for the vote of confidence."

She lifted a shoulder. "You're welcome."

Gus glanced in the rearview mirror and stiffened. They'd gotten off one major road onto another and the vehicle behind them was the same one that had been there for the past five miles. He handed his cell phone to Jane. "Call Declan—he should be the first number in my favorites. Give him a heads-up."

"Why?" Jane twisted in her seat.

He nodded toward the rearview mirror. "We might have some trouble."

JANE STARED AT the vehicle behind them, her pulse picking up.

"See that dark gray SUV back there?" Gus asked.

"Yes." The vehicle didn't appear to be dangerous. It was following approximately ten car lengths behind them. A white sedan swerved in between them.

The SUV sped up, passed the white car and pulled back in behind them, now eight vehicle lengths back.

"It's been there through the last interchange and keeping pace. When we change lanes, he changes."

"You think he's following us?" Jane hadn't been

watching the entire time but he sure appeared to be following them.

"We can find out easily enough," Gus said. "Call Declan."

Jane found Declan's number and sent the call, putting it on Speaker.

"What's up, Gus?" Declan's voice sounded loud and clear.

"Got a dark gray SUV following me for the past fifteen minutes. Wanna get off the next exit and back on to see if we shake him?"

"I'll have Grace notify Cole. Be ready to get off at the last minute."

"We'll stay on the line," Gus said.

Jane held the phone, turned sideways in the seat to better watch the vehicle behind them. She could hear voices from the interior of Declan's vehicle, Grace's voice, then Declan's and Charlie's.

"Getting off now," Declan said. Their vehicle took the next exit.

Gus waited until he'd almost passed the exit before he swerved to get off, no signal.

Jane held her breath. The dark gray SUV followed them on the off ramp. "He's sticking with us."

"We have a stoplight ahead," Declan said.

"Can you blow it without causing a wreck?" Gus asked.

More voices from Declan's vehicle.

"Blowing," Declan said.

Ahead of them, they could see Cole's SUV race through the red light, across the intersection and onto the ramp leading back onto the highway. Declan's vehicle followed.

A car coming from the other direction skidded to a stop, barely missing the rear end of the vehicle carrying Charlie and the others.

Jane gasped and held on as Gus hit his hazard lights and then his horn and followed Declan through the red light and the intersection, racing up the on-ramp leading back to the highway they'd just left.

The dark gray SUV started through the intersection and stopped when two other vehicles blocked his path.

"He got stuck at the intersection," Jane said, grinning. A moment later her grin died. "Damn."

"What?"

"He made it through the intersection and is coming up the ramp."

"We hear you," Declan said. "We'll try some evasive measures. Be ready to zip in and out of traffic."

"Following," Gus acknowledged. "Just go. We'll keep up and try to get a license plate number."

"You watch the front. I'll let you know what's going on behind us." Jane twisted more in her seat and watched out the back window for the SUV.

Gus maneuvered through several lane changes, moving ahead in the heavy traffic, a little at time.

"I don't see our tail," Jane said, squinting to see in the distance around several cars blocking her view. "No, wait—he's back there. Three vehicles between us."

More lane changes and the dark gray SUV disappeared again. "I think we lost him."

"Good. But we can't let our guard down."

"I'm watching." Jane turned in her seat, looking all around for any other signs of being followed. They passed a ramp leading off the freeway, crossed a bridge and slowed as merging traffic clogged the rest of the vehicles moving through.

Out of the corner of her eye, Jane saw a flash of dark gray metal as an SUV darted out of the merging traffic from the on-ramp and crossed two lanes of traffic, heading for them.

"Look out to the right!" Jane cried. "He's back and coming straight for us."

The dark gray SUV slammed into the side of their vehicle, crushing Jane's door inward and shoving them into the fast lane.

The car on their left swerved onto the shoulder and slammed on the breaks to let them pass, the driver laying on the horn.

Gus gripped the steering wheel, his knuckles turning white as he fought to keep the SUV from running off the road into the concrete barriers.

The dark gray SUV didn't let up, pushing them closer and closer to the concrete.

"Hold on," Gus said.

Jane leaned toward the console, holding on to the handle over the door.

Gus jerked the steering wheel to the right, pushing back on the other vehicle. He couldn't slow and let him pass because that would leave Charlie's vehicle vulnerable.

Jane tried to see into the other SUV, but the windows were so darkly tinted she couldn't make out the driver, even though they were close enough she could have spit into his window.

Gus jammed his foot onto the accelerator, continuing to steer his vehicle into the SUV. The other drivers on the road slowed, giving them space.

"You okay back there?" Declan called out over the cell phone.

"Don't slow down. Get Charlie home," Gus said through clenched teeth, his arms straining as he maintained his hold on the steering wheel.

"Going," Declan acknowledged. "Grace is calling the highway patrol. Hang in there."

Suddenly the gray SUV jerked to the right, running parallel to their vehicle.

Jane had time only to take a breath before the glass in the window beside her exploded inward, showering her with small shards.

"Damn!" Gus hit the accelerator. "Get down!"

he yelled and raced ahead of the other vehicle, ducking as low as he could.

Jane leaned low in her seat, staring up at the bullet hole in the passenger window. She followed its trajectory to Gus. Bright red blood dripped from his shoulder onto the seat.

"You're hit!" Jane cried out and started to sit up.

"Stay down, damn it!" he yelled.

The dark SUV raced up beside them again.

Gus didn't wait for the driver to start shooting again. He jerked the steering wheel to the right, slamming into the other vehicle. Then he goosed the accelerator and shot in front of the gray SUV, blocking the driver from coming up again on the side. When he tried to go around, Gus planted his vehicle in the way every time.

Jane risked a look over the back of the seat in time to see the driver stick a gun out the window, aimed at the back of their SUV. "Look out—he's going to shoot at the back."

Jane ducked low again, just in time. A bullet hit the back windshield and exited the vehicle through the front. If she hadn't ducked, it would have gone through her head.

"Brace yourself," Gus shouted.

Jane didn't know what to hold on to. She grabbed the armrest and gripped tight.

Gus jammed on the brakes, bringing the SUV to a skidding stop in the middle of the freeway.

The driver behind him hit his brakes, but too late to stop before slamming into the back of their SUV.

Jane was flung forward; her seat belt tightened, keeping her from flying through the windshield and out onto the pavement.

Gus let off the brake and hit the accelerator, racing ahead of the gray SUV.

Jane glanced back to see steam rising from the hood of the other vehicle. It wasn't moving. As the distance increased between them, her heartbeat slowed and she took a breath. She stared across at Gus whose arm was bleeding. "Get to the nearest hospital. You've got a gunshot wound."

"I'm fine. It just grazed me."

"Grazing doesn't bleed that much." She searched the interior of the vehicle for napkins or tissues to use to stop the flow of blood. When she couldn't find any, she pressed her palm against the wound, applying pressure. "Seriously, you're bleeding like a stuck pig. At least go to a convenient care clinic and get some stitches."

"When we get to the estate, I'll ask for a Band-Aid."

She sighed. "You're hopeless."

He shot her a grin. "And you're doing great. Most women I've known would have fainted at the sight of blood."

"You've known the wrong women. I'm not most women," she grumbled.

His grin faded, but his look was intense. "No. You're not."

"I hope you didn't get blood on my finger-print card. We still need to find out what kind of woman I am."

Chapter Nine

Gus made it back to Charlie's place without bleeding out. With Jane applying pressure all the way, she'd pretty much stopped the flow by the time they arrived.

The others were standing outside the mansion on the steps when Gus pulled in behind their vehicles.

Declan hurried forward. "Ho-ly… Gus. Are you okay?"

As soon as he shifted into Park, he took over from Jane and pressed his hand over the wound on his shoulder. "I'm fine."

"If you're so fine, why are you bleeding like a stuck pig?" Cole asked.

"What's with people and stuck pigs?" Gus shook his head. "All I need is a shower and a Band-Aid. It's just a flesh wound."

"I'm calling my doctor," Charlie announced.

She had her cell phone out and was dialing before Gus could tell her he didn't need one.

"It's just a flesh wound," he insisted.

"Let the doctor be the judge of that," Charlie said as she ended the call. "He'll be here in ten minutes."

"Your doctor makes house calls?" Mustang asked.

"For me," Charlie said. "I set him up in his own practice just down the road. He returns the favor on occasion. I don't abuse the privilege, only when I think it's necessary. And I think it's necessary based on the amount of blood you have all over you and Jane. Come on—let's get you inside and cleaned up."

"I'll grab some clean towels and gauze." Arnold hurried up the steps ahead of them.

"I'll get the alcohol," Cole said.

"Shouldn't he wash the wound first?" Charlie asked.

Cole shot a grin back at the others as he stepped through the door. "I'll leave that to Gus. I'm getting the beer and whiskey."

Declan shook his head and turned to Gus. "You sure you're all right?"

"Seriously, it's just a flesh wound," Gus said.

Declan snorted. "You'd say that if half your arm was blown off."

Gus chuckled. "Probably. And you'd do the same."

"Yeah." Declan grinned. "And Cole would get the booze."

"While you guys are being guys, Gus is still bleeding." Jane wrapped her arm around Gus's waist and looped his arm over her shoulders.

"What are you doing?" Gus asked.

"You've lost a lot of blood, cowboy. I'm going to make sure you get up the steps without passing out." Jane started up the stairs.

He frowned down at her. "I've never passed out a day in my life."

"Then do it yourself," she said and started to duck out from under his arm.

He held on tight. "No. I think you're right. I'm feeling a little fuzzy."

"Come on, cowboy," Declan said, shaking his head. "Let's get inside before you stain the concrete and marble."

Gus leaned a little more than he should have on Jane, but he liked her arm around his waist and that she cared enough to help him up the stairs. He didn't need the help and he didn't feel at all woozy. He wasn't going to tell her that. She wouldn't believe him anyway. It looked like he'd lost a lot of blood, but he really hadn't.

"Can you make it up to the second floor?" Charlie asked. "You can use the shower in my room."

"Not necessary. I can make it to the third floor just fine."

"Great," Jane said, already breathing hard.

He stopped leaning so heavily on her but let her keep her arm around his waist. "Better?"

"Much." She frowned up at him. "Faker."

"I told you I didn't need the help." He leaned close to her ear. "Don't blame me if I liked it."

"Jerk," she muttered and continued up the stairs with her arm around his waist.

Once they made it to the suite they shared, she walked him straight to the bathroom before she ducked from beneath his arm to reach in and turn the knob on the shower.

When the water was nice and warm, she turned back to find him pulling his T-shirt over his head. The wound on his arm started bleeding again, dripping onto the floor.

"You could have waited for me to help," she groused.

"Why? It was going to bleed anyway." He pressed the T-shirt to the wound.

"Hold that thought while I untie your boots." She leaned down and loosened the laces on his boots.

He toed them off.

She helped him remove his socks and then straightened.

He touched her cheek with the hand on his injured arm, leaving a streak of blood. "You're pretty handy to have around when a guy is bleeding. Sorry, I just left some on your face."

"Shut up and let me maintain the pressure while you get out of those jeans."

"You sure you want to do that?"

"I'd rather hold the wound than have you slip and break your neck in your own blood." She held the shirt against the injury. "I'll even close my eyes."

Just the thought of getting naked with her made his blood pump faster and his desire swell in his groin. "I don't think it's a good idea."

She glared up at him. "I repeat. Shut up and do it." Then she closed her eyes.

While she held his arm, he slipped out of his jeans, pulled the shower curtain over to cover himself and then clamped his hand over the wound. "Okay, I've got this now. You can go."

"I'll stay long enough to help you out. Once you wash all the blood off, you'll need help getting dressed without messing up your clean clothes."

He hadn't thought of that, when all he could think about was the effect she was having on his libido. "You make a good point. But I'm not sure I want your help."

She frowned. "Do you want me to get one of your teammates? I can do that."

He didn't like that idea either. "No. I suppose you'll do."

Jane shook her head. "Ingrate. Move. The doctor will be here to sew you up any minute."

"Maybe we should have waited for him before doing the shower."

"You're a mess. Get in the shower before all the hot water is gone."

"Yes, ma'am." He stepped behind the curtain.

A hand came around the side of the curtain with a clean washcloth. "Use this to apply pressure to the wound and just let the water wash over your body. You can get a better shower after the doc sews you up."

He stopped short of asking her to wash the blood away from his body. If he weren't her guard and she weren't an unknown potential threat, he might have done it. He reached down and turned the shower cooler.

The woman was getting to him more than he cared to admit. His body had no problem demonstrating its desire for her.

"Are you okay in there?" Jane's voice sounded from the other side of the curtain.

"I'm fine," he said through gritted teeth. The water was damned cold, yet it did little to get his desire in check.

"I found some shorts in your gym bag. Where do you keep your underwear?"

He chuckled. "I don't."

"You don't what?" she asked.

"I don't keep them."

"Oh."

Gus smiled, imagining the look on her face when she understood that he went commando whenever he could. When he couldn't he wore boxer shorts.

Holding the cloth over his wound, he let the water sluice over his body, washing away as much of the blood as he could see. When he was clean, he turned off the water.

A towel flew over the curtain rod and slapped him in the face.

"Thanks," he said.

"You're welcome."

He could see the outline of her body standing near the curtain.

"Need help drying off?" she asked.

"No. I've got this." He managed to get to most of the water, patting himself dry.

"I'll step out and let you get into your shorts."

"Mighty decent of you, ma'am," he said in his best imitation of John Wayne.

"Don't give up your day job, Gus," she said and pulled the door closed as she left.

Gus tugged on his shorts while holding the cloth in place. He barely had them covering all the important parts when Jane stuck her head through the door. "The doctor's here."

Thankful for the distraction, Gus left the bathroom to find a young man carrying a black satchel. The guy barely looked old enough to be out of medical school.

"I'm thirty-five years old," the doctor said as he set his bag on an end table near an ottoman. "I happen to have a young face. But I'm good at what I do." He glanced toward Jane. "Can I get a towel or two to spread out over this seat?"

Jane nodded and hurried back into the bathroom, returning with a stack of clean towels. She spread two over the ottoman and stood back.

The doctor pointed. "Sit."

Gus did as he was told. The doctor might look young, but he worked quickly and efficiently, examining the wound and applying three sutures to close the edges.

"When was your last tetanus shot?" he asked.

"I don't know. Maybe five years ago," Gus said.

After the doctor applied gauze and tape to cover the wound, he gave Gus a shot, some antibiotics and then he closed his case. "As far as I'm concerned, you've suffered a bad abrasion." He gave instructions for wound care and left.

"Not much of a bedside manner," Jane said, as she inspected the doctor's handiwork. "But he did a good job."

"And he's not reporting it to the authorities as a gunshot wound. We don't have time for the red tape." Gus raised an eyebrow. "Satisfied? I'm sure

I could have applied a couple of butterfly bandages and been just as effective."

Jane rolled her eyes and held out a T-shirt. "Want help getting into this?"

He sighed. "Is there no end to the humiliation?"

"Stop being a baby and put on the shirt. I'm sure you don't want to sit at the dinner table shirtless."

He didn't, so he let her help him into the shirt.

"You kinda need a shower. You have almost as much blood on you as I had on me."

She nodded toward the door. "If you want to go down and join the others, I'll get that shower."

"Have you forgotten that I'm supposed to be keeping an eye on you?"

Jane sighed. "Whatever. I'm getting a shower. Do what you want. I'm not going to make a run for it when Carl said he had a big pot of Hungarian goulash on the stove. I can smell it all the way up here." She inhaled deeply. "Nope. I won't make a run for it until I've had some of that."

She collected clothes from her bedroom, took them into the bathroom and closed the door between them.

Gus stood on the other side, every instinct telling him that she was one of the good guys and that he could trust her. In which case, he wouldn't have to treat her like a potential threat. He could explore this reaction he had to her nearness.

If she was willing.

He heard when she turned on the water.

His imagination pictured her naked, standing beneath the spray, water sluicing down over her shoulders and breasts. He could be in there, rubbing soap over her skin, sliding his hands over every inch of her body.

Gus groaned. Why was he torturing himself?

The water turned off, but Gus was still turned on.

"Gus?" Jane called out.

He thought he'd imagined it.

"Gus?" The second time, she was louder.

His pulse quickened and he hurried to the bathroom door, opening it a crack. "Yeah."

"I forgot to get a towel out of the cabinet. Would you hand me one?" Jane stood on the other side of the curtain, her naked body a hazy gray silhouette.

"Sure." He reached into the cabinet and pulled out a fluffy white towel. He slipped it around the side of the shower curtain and she took it from him.

"Thanks."

"You're welcome," he said, choking on his desire.

He made it to the door when the shower curtain whipped to the side.

He glanced back over his shoulder.

She stood, wrapped in the towel, water droplets gleaming off the swells of her breasts. "I'll be ready in a minute."

Gus dove for the door. He was ready now, but not for Hungarian goulash.

AFTER GUS LEFT her alone in the bathroom, Jane rubbed her body dry with the towel he'd given her.

The whole time she'd helped him undress and get into the shower she'd fought the overwhelming urge to get in with him. It would have been easier for him, if she had. But what purpose would it serve? The man made her blood burn hot through her veins. When he'd stripped down to get into the shower she'd done her best not to peek, but damn. He was one hell of a male specimen.

She'd slept in his arms the night before and felt the strength of his muscles and the heat of his skin against hers and wished for a lot more than being held. But she couldn't ask for more. It wouldn't be fair to him. Making love to her wasn't part of his job duties.

Oh, but what she wouldn't give to have his hands on her body, touching her from head to toe. How long had it been since she'd been with a man? Hell, she had no idea. Frustration burned a hole in her gut.

Jane finished drying her body and wrapped her hair in the towel to soak up the water. She slipped into the panties and bra Grace had loaned her. Then she pulled on a soft red jersey dress. It slipped down over her body, hugging every curve and swell, falling all the way to her ankles. She couldn't remember wearing a dress. Did she do it often? Or was it a new experience?

The shoes Grace had given her to wear with the dress were high heels. After the day she'd had, Jane had no desire to wear spike heels, deciding instead to go barefoot.

She hung the towel on a rack and pulled a brush through her hair.

The thought of Gus waiting in the other room made her want to hurry to see his reaction to the red dress. It wasn't as fancy as the black one she'd worn to the gala, but it suited her more. She felt comfortable, yet feminine wearing it.

Once she'd smoothed all the tangles from her long hair she stepped out of the bathroom.

Gus stood by the French doors. He'd changed from the shorts into a pair of black jeans and a pair of leather boots. He still wore the T-shirt she'd helped him into and his hair was combed back from his forehead.

Dark stubble peppered his chin, giving him a more dangerous appearance.

He turned toward her, his eyes widening briefly as he took in her form in the dress.

"You clean up nicely," he said.

Her lips quirked. "You're not so bad yourself."

"And I managed to dress myself," he said, puffing out his chest.

"Now that you're not bleeding," she reminded him.

"Thanks to you," he said. He crossed the room to stand in front of her.

She stared up at his face, her gaze dropping to his full lips, curious to know if they were as soft as they looked. Was he a good kisser?

Her stomach rumbled, pulling her back to reality. Heat rose in her cheeks and she pressed a hand to her belly. "I suppose we should go downstairs."

He nodded and tipped her chin up. "Thank you for taking care of me when you didn't have to."

"You're welcome," she said, her voice barely more than a whisper.

Gus's head dipped lower. "I have an uncontrollable desire to kiss you."

Her breath caught and her heartbeat ratcheted up. "What's stopping you?"

"I can't think of a damned thing." He lowered his mouth to hers, brushing a feather-soft kiss across her lips.

She sighed, leaning up on her toes to deepen the connection.

Gus's arms wrapped around her, bringing her body flush up against his. When his tongue traced the seam of her lips, she opened to him and met him thrust for thrust.

The moment lasted forever and was over in a second.

He lifted his head and she wanted to cry for the loss of his lips on hers.

Leaning her forehead against his chest, she whispered, "We should go down."

"In a perfect world, I'd say to hell with that and keep you up here in our own little suite and kiss you again."

She lifted her head and stared up into eyes so dark with passion they made her burn for him. "What's stopping you?"

He breathed in and out again as if steadying himself before answering. "We aren't alone in this house. The others will be expecting us to come down soon."

Jane nodded. "Then let's go."

He cupped her chin and lifted her face to his. "Tonight." He spoke the one word like a promise.

A shiver of excitement rippled through her. "Tonight," she repeated.

Gus extended his arm to her and she looped her hand through his elbow.

They walked all the way down the stairs before she let go and preceded him into the kitchen.

As they strode into the room every member of Declan's Defenders turned toward them, their gazes intense, all frowning.

A lead weight settled in the pit of Jane's belly.

"What?" Gus asked.

"Mack and Snow?" Declan turned to them.

Mack focused on Gus. "Our trip to Langley was enlightening."

Snow continued. "Apparently, the CIA has been tracking certain people who have had dealings with the Russians and the Syrian rebels." Snow's gaze shifted from Gus to Jane.

"And?" Gus raised a hand to the small of Jane's back.

She moved away from him so that his hand fell to his side. She didn't want his marine brothers to think he had anything to do with her, other than his responsibility to keep an eye on her. What they had to say wasn't going to be good. Gus didn't need to be associated with her if she was purely bad.

"What did you find out?" Gus prompted impatiently.

Declan looked to Snow. "We think we know who Jane is."

Jane's heart raced and her pulse pounded so hard against her eardrums she could barely hear.

"Spit it out, damn it," Gus said through gritted teeth.

"It's okay," Jane said. "Whatever you have to say, I need to hear." She stood with her shoulders back, her chin held high.

"The CIA has been tracking a secret agent who goes by the code name Indigo."

"Are you telling me our Jane Doe is Indigo?" Gus demanded.

"She fits the description," Mack said. "Dark hair, dark eyes."

"That could be any woman in Syria," Gus argued.

"Speaks several languages," Snow continued.

"Again, that could be a number of people in Syria," Gus said.

Jane touched his arm. "It's okay. I need to know."

"There's a reason she's a skilled fighter," Mack said, his eyes narrowing as his gaze shot to Jane. "She's a trained assassin."

Chapter Ten

Gus flinched as if he'd been punched in the gut.

Jane? His Jane? A trained assassin?

She stood beside him, her face pale, her eyes rounded.

"Any of this coming back to you?" Mack asked.

She shook her head. "No."

"I can't believe it," Gus said. "She can't be a trained assassin."

"I have my guy at Langley searching files for images." Mack shifted his gaze from Jane back to Gus. "They will contact me as soon as they have something."

Gus shoved a hand through his hair and stared at his friend and teammate. "How did you approach the subject of Jane? Did you tell them she was here? With us?"

"No. Actually, they don't know we have anyone. We went on a mission to find out more about what's going on in Syria. We asked if there were persons of interest they were following who could be a danger to the US."

Gus shook his head. "And they jumped right to this Indigo person?"

"No, they had a list of Russian spies, Syrian rebels and mercenaries for hire."

He wasn't buying into Jane being Indigo, but he had to know how the assassin fit in. "Which group does Indigo have allegiance to?"

Mack's lips pressed into a tight line. "That's just it—she doesn't claim any of the groups. They think someone is using her to orchestrate his own agenda."

"What agenda did the CIA come up with?" Gus crossed his arms over his chest.

Snow answered. "A high-ranking Russian military leader, Lieutenant General Mikhail Marouchevsky, was assassinated minutes before he was due to evacuate the Shayrat Airbase. All the Russian planes made it out before the US bombed the airfield. All the Russians survived, except the lieutenant general."

"If they thought I was this Indigo assassin, that would explain why the guards beating me spoke Russian," Jane said. "They were dressed like Syrian rebels, but they spoke Russian and carried Russian AK-47s."

Charlie's eyes rounded. "Your tattoo led you

here." She pressed her hand to her mouth. "Could you be…" She shook her head. "No."

"Your husband's assassin?" Jane's face turned even another shade paler.

"This is all circumstantial," Gus said. "Jane might not even be this Indigo assassin."

"Does the CIA know of others like her?" Grace asked. "Are any of them marked with the Trinity knot?"

"Who do we know so far who has had a connection to the symbol?" Declan said.

Charlie's brow furrowed. "My husband had a ring with that symbol on it."

"My friend Riley's nanny had that symbol on a similar ring," Grace said. "And she was a Russian sleeper spy, living in the US."

"Now we have Jane, who speaks Russian and Arabic," Declan said. "Coincidence?" He shook his head. "I think not."

"But what would my husband have to do with an organization that employees Russian sleeper spies and trained assassins?" Charlie slipped into a chair at the kitchen table and buried her face in her hands. "Oh, John, what were you into?"

"All the more reason to break into his files." Cole stood. "He had to know something about what tied them all together. Maybe I can find some information on the Dark Web."

"Be careful. You open yourself up to all kinds of fanatics when you go there," Declan warned.

Cole nodded. "I'll be sure to set up a special IP address and mask it to maintain anonymity."

Charlie stared at Jane and finally shook her head. "No. I can't even conceive of the idea that Jane was the assassin behind my husband's murder. She wouldn't have done it. She's had ample opportunity to harm any one of us since staying here, and she's done nothing but help instead."

Gus felt the same way. But what if he was wrong?

"Mrs. Halverson, I pray I didn't," Jane said. "If your husband was anything like you, I couldn't have killed him. You are a good person, with a heart willing to take in the strays and help those in need. The world needs more people like you, not fewer."

Charlie gave her a weak smile. "Thank you, dear." She looked around the room at the others. "I'm not giving up on Jane. If she is Indigo, what proof do we have that she's assassinated anyone? If she's not Indigo, we still have to discover who she is. Don't stop searching yet."

Mack nodded, his gaze on Jane. "In the meantime, what do we do with Jane?"

"I won't promise not to hurt you, because you probably wouldn't believe me. If I am truly the assassin Indigo, even assassins can turn over a new leaf. I don't have to be an assassin, if I don't want to. And I really don't want to." She looked around at the doubting faces. "The other alternative is to kick me out."

Gus's gut clenched. Though he hadn't wanted to be her guard, now it seemed he didn't want the job to end.

When Charlie shook her head and opened her mouth to say something, Jane held up her hand. "It's okay if you do. I've probably overstayed my welcome, as it is." She looked around at the men of Declan's Defenders, their boss, Charlie, Arnold the butler, Carl the cook and Grace, Charlie's assistant. "You are a family. I'm the outsider."

Gus felt a hard tug at his heart. A family was all he'd ever wanted. And quite possibly, it was all Jane wanted, too. He could hear the hollowness in her voice, the hopelessness of her situation.

"I don't suppose any of you want to eat after all that?" Carl asked softly.

Jane's stomach rumbled loudly. She pressed a hand to it. "I only ask that you don't kick me out until I've had at least a taste of Carl's goulash." She faked a laugh, though it sounded more like a sob.

Gus was almost certain assassins didn't cry.

Charlie drew in a shaky breath and crossed the floor to Jane, pulling her into a tight hug. "I don't believe you killed John. There has to be another reason that tattoo is on your wrist, and that it led you here. And we'll find it." She pushed Jane to arm's length and stared into her eyes. "I promise."

Gus let go of the breath he'd been holding. Charlie had every right to boot Jane out of her home. Hell, if they thought she was Indigo, they had an obligation to turn her over to the CIA for questioning. None of them stepped forward with that suggestion.

Instead, they gathered around the kitchen table and filled their bowls full of Carl's Hungarian goulash and ate a hearty meal.

Gus sat beside Jane. At one point, he laid his hand over hers where she rested it in her lap.

She glanced his way and then looked away, moving her hand from beneath his.

He'd meant to reassure her that he was there for her. Was she already letting go?

He hadn't known her long, but what he'd seen of her was enough to make him want to spend more time with her. She was strong, determined and capable of taking care of herself. But it was the vulnerable side that drew him even more.

He hoped the CIA was wrong about Indigo being his Jane. But if she was in fact Indigo… hell, he wasn't sure what he'd do then.

Jane rolled the name Indigo over and over in her mind. It didn't kick off any bells or alarms. In fact, it didn't sound right to her ears. Perhaps it wasn't a name she used for herself. But if not Indigo or

Jane, what name fit? She wanted to bury her face in her hands and weep.

An assassin?

She ate the goulash, savoring every last bite as if it might be her last meal. And the way things were shaping up, it just might.

When the platter of rolls was passed to her, she grabbed two, setting one on the table beside her plate. She'd wrap it in a napkin and take it with her when Charlie got smart and asked her to leave.

The usual lighthearted humor was absent from the table.

Snow shot a glance toward Declan. "What happened to the SUV out front?"

Gus told him about the run-in they had with another SUV on the freeway.

Mack tilted his head slightly. "The entire time he was after you, did he even try to get past your vehicle to Charlie's?"

Gus thought about it. The dark gray SUV had a couple of opportunities to race past them and attack Charlie's car. "No. He never tried."

"Could it be whoever was attacking your vehicle might have been going after Jane?" Snow pointed out.

"Why would he?" Declan asked. "*We* don't even know who Jane is. How would anyone else? The only people who know she's here are in this room."

Gus shook his head. "That's not exactly true."

"Gus is right," Charlie said. "She was at the gala when Charlie was attacked. And we went by Halverson International Headquarters. She was seen by any number of people, from security guards to receptionists."

"Don't forget your husband's executive assistant, Margaret, and your CEO, Quincy Phishburn," Cole added.

"Do you think someone in the Halverson headquarters knows about Jane?" Charlie asked.

"Could be." Declan tapped his chin. "The question is why would they want to run her off the road?"

"Obviously, to kill her," Gus said, his food lodging halfway to his stomach.

"Yes, but why would they want to kill her?" Declan continued. "Who knows she's an assassin?" He gave Jane a crooked smile. "Assuming you are."

She shrugged.

"Someone who knows about her and what happened in Syria?" Mack suggested.

"Someone who doesn't want anyone to know what happened in Syria," Gus guessed.

"All the more reason to get to the bottom of who Jane is and why someone is after her." Charlie shook her head. "I just assumed the vehicle following you was ultimately after me. That's what I get for assuming."

After the meal was complete, Jane approached

Charlie. "Do you want me to leave?" she asked quietly so that no one else could hear. She wanted Charlie to have the opportunity to cut her losses and let her go without the pressure of everyone watching or judging.

Charlie shook her head adamantly. "Absolutely not."

"What if I'm the assassin who killed your husband?"

"You're not." Charlie patted her arm. "I'm completely convinced of that. You could have hurt us all by now, as I said, if you are an assassin. I doubt you would have wasted so much time just to gain our trust. It doesn't make sense. You didn't kill John."

"You won't hurt my feelings if you want me to go. I'd have kicked me out long ago if I were you."

Charlie smiled. "Then it's a good thing you're not me. I have a feeling John would have wanted us to help you. He was that kind of man. He helped people who needed it. Given all the information we have thus far, I'm sure he wouldn't have kicked you out, either."

"Thank you, Charlie. I hope you don't come to regret your decision."

"I won't. And we're going to figure out this mess. You'll see. Everything will turn out right in the end."

Jane wished that was so.

Until they reached the end, she vowed to walk a very straight-and-narrow line so that her mere presence among Declan's Defenders didn't make the men nervous.

Charlie stared at Jane, her brow dipping low as she swept her gaze over the younger woman. "We need to get you to town and buy some clothes that fit."

"I'm fine with what Grace provided."

"The red dress is lovely, but you need other items of your own, like jeans. Two women can't wear the same pair of jeans. We're all built so differently." Charlie looked past Jane. "Arnold, tomorrow we'll need the car brought out around nine o'clock in the morning."

Arnold nodded. "Yes, ma'am."

Jane shook her head. "I don't want to bother you, Charlie."

"You're not a bother. It's settled—we're going shopping in the morning." She glanced toward Declan. "We'll need coverage to make the trip into town."

"We're on it," Declan assured her.

"Have you finished searching John's things?" Charlie asked.

"Not yet," Declan answered. "While Cole and Jonah work on digital data, we'll search the entire house."

"Not just the house," Charlie said. "We purchased this estate from a retired FBI agent. He had all kinds of secret hiding places and passages. I think he was a little paranoid."

"We'll search everywhere," Declan said. "I know about the underground passageway to the garage. Are there more?"

"Yes. I believe there's one to the garden," Charlie said. "There might be some hidden rooms behind the walls here in the house and garage. I'm not certain I know where all of them are. John might have found some I didn't."

"Don't forget the fingerprint card we made with Jane's prints," Gus reminded Cole.

"Got it," Cole said. "We'll work on that first."

"What do you know about the IAFIS system?" Gus asked.

"Enough to find matching prints in the criminal, military and government databases. Why?" Cole asked.

"If you find a match, can someone be automatically notified if they're looking for that person?"

Cole's brow knit. "I'm not sure I follow."

"If someone is looking for that person and another investigator finds a match, will the original searcher get notification of that match? I don't want anyone to know where to find Jane, if we get a hit."

That Gus was concerned for her well-being made Jane's heart swell.

"Good point," Cole said. "I'll be sure to route it so that the inquiry doesn't show up any IP address associated with Halverson estate."

"Good," Declan said. "We don't need to bring any more trouble to Charlie's doorstep than we already have."

Was that it? The warmth Jane had experienced over Gus's concern for her cooled. He was worried about bringing the bad guys here.

When had Jane started thinking everything was about her? She should know better. If she wanted to be protected, she had to take care of herself. She was already thinking of where she could go, if her location was compromised. Staying with Charlie wouldn't be an option. The woman didn't deserve to have more threats dropped at her door.

They split up, assigning different areas of the house and grounds for each person to search.

Gus and Jane took the third floor and attic since they were rooming up there anyway.

They felt their way around every wall in every room on the third floor; they touched wall sconces, moved furniture and checked beneath rugs. Nothing jumped out at them and no walls opened up magically to reveal a hidden room.

Narrow stairs led up into the attic. A fine layer of dust coated the contents of the space. Some of the items appeared to have been there from the previous owner. Cardboard boxes were stacked in several corners along with old furniture and lamps. A single yellow light bulb lit the space, albeit inadequately. As they moved around the attic, dust rose with every step, making it even murkier than before they entered. The light reflected off the particles of dust, giving it a hazy surreal atmosphere.

Jane shivered, not liking the feeling of the place. The dust reminded her of the dirt floor in her Syrian cell. The sooner she got out of there the better.

"I don't see anything up here," Gus said. "Let's go to the ground floor. Maybe there's a secret cupboard off the subterranean conference room below Mr. Halverson's office."

Glad to be out of the attic, Jane hurried downstairs.

Declan met them halfway down on the second floor. "Anything?"

Gus shook his head. "We even tapped on the walls and listened for anything that sounded hollow."

"Same here," Declan said. "We checked every room except Charlie's. Grace is helping her go through it now."

"We thought we might look in the subterranean conference room." Gus followed Jane down the steps, Declan close behind. "Perhaps there's a hidden door we haven't noticed."

Declan nodded. "It would make sense, since the conference room is more or less hidden beneath Halverson's old office." When they reached the ground floor, Declan fell in beside Gus. "I'm surprised Halverson didn't involve his wife more in what he was doing."

"He might not have wanted her to be so close to the truth of what he was doing that she'd become a target."

Jane snorted. "She lived with the man. Isn't that close enough? Don't you think the attacks could be continuations of the effort to end whatever John Halverson was doing? They might think Charlie is just as involved."

"True. All the more reason for full disclosure," Declan said. "We need to know just what John Halverson was dealing with."

"We could go through his office again," Jane said. "We might be missing something." She so desperately wanted to find anything that would help her to understand why she had been led to Halverson's estate. What did he have to do with the Trinity symbols? Was he involved with an organization that used the Trinity knot as a sign? Or was he investigating such an organization in an attempt to bring it down?

What was the Trinity organization and what was it involved with? Did they hire out like mercenaries to assassinate for a paycheck? Was that why she'd been in Syria?

God, she hoped not. She prayed she wasn't an

assassin for hire. That the intel had been wrong. She wasn't a cold-blooded killer. She didn't feel like it was in her nature to kill unnecessarily.

"I'm going out to the garage via the access tunnel to help Snow search there." Declan nodded toward Halverson's study. "Good luck. We didn't find anything when we went through the files and drawers. But then a second pair of eyes is always a good thing."

Alone in the office with Gus, Jane couldn't help glancing his way. Before they'd discovered she could be a trained assassin, he'd kissed her and left her with a vague promise of more that night. Would he carry through with that promise, now that he knew she might be a ruthless assassin?

Jane didn't hold out any hope of that happening. A man would have to be crazy to consort with someone like her.

She ran her fingers along the top of John Halverson's desk, searching for any recessed buttons or switches that would open the desk like the one at corporate headquarters. The desktop was all smooth mahogany, not a bump or crevice anywhere on its shiny surface.

Squatting in front of the desk, she tried to think like a man who had things to hide. She felt along the underside of the surface for any indentations that would fit a finger. Again, she found nothing. Studying the overall construction of the massive desk, she realized the drawers didn't start until a good six inches below the desktop. The wood above it was an intricate, inlaid panel of highly polished mahogany with carved designs that appeared to be a kind of latticework of vines crisscrossing over each other. She touched the pattern, feeling along the raised carving all the way to the corner. Her fingers pressed into the corner and it moved outward. When it moved, the rest of the inlaid design dropped forward on hinges and a thin shelflike drawer popped out.

Jane jerked up so fast, she bumped her head on the desktop.

Gus turned from the fireplace mantel he'd been running his fingers across. "Hey, are you okay over there?"

"I think I found something," she said, rubbing the top of her head. She rose up to stand, looking down at the shallow drawer. Inside was a journal, flat enough to fit in the small space. She lifted it out of the drawer and laid it on the desk's surface.

Gus joined her as she opened the journal and read the words on the first page.

"The Trinity Syndicate."

A cold chill rippled down the back of Jane's spine and a heavy feeling settled deep in her belly.

She turned the page and read what appeared to be a diary written by John Halverson about his investigation into the inner workings of the organization called The Trinity Syndicate.

He'd first learned of the group when a potential presidential candidate was killed in a freak hunting accident during the primaries. Though the police couldn't prove it was anything more than an accident, rumors spread that the candidate had been murdered, the murderer having staged it so it didn't appear deliberate.

John hadn't thought much of it then, but when a bombing occurred in a government building, everyone assumed it was a product of Taliban terrorism. True, the vehicle used to carry the bomb and left in the underground garage had been driven by a man associated with the Taliban, but the type of bomb was much too complicated and intricate to be something generally associated with the Taliban brand of terrorism.

A German delegate to the European Union who opposed lifting sanctions against Russia was believed to have committed suicide by jumping from a bridge onto a deserted stretch of the Autobahn in the middle of the night. Though an autopsy was conducted, there wasn't much left to look at after his body had been run over by several large delivery trucks before anyone realized it was a human body in the middle of the road.

One page after another detailed incidents deemed accidents or terrorist activities that John believed were in fact orchestrated by The Trinity Syndicate to cause different outcomes in political arenas.

Near the middle of the journal, John had sketched a diagram that caught and held Jane's attention and made her heart thud against her ribs.

In effect, the diagram was an organization chart with code names at each level. At the bottom of one of the tree branches was the name Indigo.

Chapter Eleven

Gus stared down at the name on the page. He could feel Jane stiffen and hear the sharp intake of breath.

"We don't know that you are that person," he reminded her.

"What if I am?"

"We deal with it. Until then, you can't worry about it."

"Oh, but I can," she whispered.

"Declan! Mack! Gus! Snow! Anyone!" Cole's voice came through the open door in the wall of the study that led down into the basement conference room. "You gotta see this!"

Declan appeared in the doorway to the study, Mack close behind him. "Is that Cole?"

Gus nodded, grabbed the journal and hurried down the stairs into the room below the study.

Cole sat at a desk with an array of six monitors arranged in two rows of three each attached to the wall.

Jonah Spradlin sat beside him, staring at the different screens, shaking his head. "Wow. Look at it all."

Gus, Jane and the others all crowded around behind Cole.

"What are we looking at?" Declan asked.

"I'm on the Dark Web. I got a tip to look in a certain location and found all of this." He waved a hand toward the monitors.

One screen played a video of children in their preteens and teens wearing tattered dirty-white martial arts shirts and pants. Their heads were shaved whether they were boys or girls and they were being yelled at by a man with an equally shaved head. He instructed them on the proper way to take a man down and snap his neck. The children were then paired off to practice the moves up to the snapping of the neck. When one failed to perform it properly, he or she was beaten with a horse-riding crop.

Jane tensed. With every blow, she winced, feeling the child's pain as if it were her own.

"And look at this." Jonah pointed at a screen of newspaper articles about children whose parents had passed away and how they were being placed in foster care. Then the foster parents were charged with child neglect when the children ran away or disappeared.

Pictures of the missing children were displayed on milk cartons and in newspapers. Beside the child's milk-carton photo was another of a similar child in appearance with the shaved head and white outfit of the Trinity recruits.

"They're stealing children," Grace said from behind Declan.

Cole nodded, his lips forming a tight line. "And forcing them into their training programs."

"John would never have been involved in something like that," Charlie said. "He loved children, even though we never had any. He would have done everything in his power to help them."

Gus held up the journal. "I think that's exactly what he was trying to do."

Charlie took the book from his hands and opened it to the first page. "Where did you find this?" she said, her voice cracking. "That's John's handwriting."

"It was in a secret drawer in his desk," Jane said.

As Charlie turned the pages, Declan and the others peered over her shoulders. When she got to the organization chart, she gasped and looked up at Jane.

Jane nodded in acknowledgement. "He knew about Indigo."

"We don't know if that's you or not," Charlie said.

"Based on the diagram, he was trying to determine the names of those in charge at each of the levels of the organization."

"Indigo is the bottom of the pyramid, a soldier on the front lines," Snow said. "She followed orders of the person above her."

"And that would be the guy with the code name Mule." Gus pointed to the next level on the diagram. "His handler is Wolf and the top of the food chain is Asp."

Charlie turned the page to the next journal entry. "He found Indigo." She looked up into Jane's eyes.

Jane moved closer to the book and read the words written in bold black ink.

I learned of the next operation Trinity had planned to initiate their operator Indigo. Buried in the Dark Web I understood this to be her first assignment, the one she needed to prove herself and her loyalty to the syndicate. Her tasking was to kill a Saudi crown prince. This particular prince was known for frequenting brothels where young girls were kept as sex slaves in the back alleys of the Bronx. This Saudi prince was also known for selling Russian secrets to the Chinese. Apparently, the Russians were willing to pay a hefty sum to have that information leak fixed.

I flew to NYC, dressed as a homeless man and lay in the alley near the entrance to the brothel waiting for the crown prince to show. He did, with three of his bodyguards, just as the informant on the Dark Web said he would. He was inside for over an hour when he finally emerged, with all three of his men surrounding him.

I never saw her slip into the alley, but suddenly Indigo was there. She wore a tight dress and spike heels with enough makeup to make her look like a street whore. When she walked up to the prince, he thought he was going to get a little more action. He made a grab for her breasts.

She barely blinked before she punched him in the throat, crushing his trachea. The prince clutched at his throat, unable to breathe past the blockage.

The three bodyguards, caught unawares, tried to capture her, but she was too fast. In some incredible martial arts moves, she had all three men flat out on the ground and unconscious in under a minute. Meanwhile the prince's face turned blue and he dropped to the ground, lying perfectly still.

Indigo bent to feel for a pulse. When she

was satisfied there was none, she straightened and entered the brothel.

That's when I knew she was different. She wasn't just a trained assassin. She'd probably broken all the rules of her training by not leaving as soon as she'd completed her mission.

I waited, hoping her handler would appear and I'd have another link in the chain of command. If I wanted to stop the assembly line of child conscription, I had to find the leader.

Her handler never appeared. A few minutes later, Indigo emerged from the brothel, carrying one young unconscious girl over her shoulder and leading a dozen others. Indigo's face was bloodied, but the men inside hadn't stopped her. She got those girls out.

I followed her to the nearest hospital where she left the unconscious girl and the dozen others at the entrance to the ER. She stopped an older couple on their way in and asked them to send help outside for the girls. When they said they would, she waited a few moments longer with the girls. As nurses and orderlies emerged to help, Indigo disappeared into the shadows.

I heard later that the men running the brothel had been critically injured and wouldn't be in the business of selling young girls for sex ever again. I made certain the girls had the care they needed to wean them off the drugs, and legal assistance to lead them through the red tape of immigration.

Charlie sniffed, a fat tear rolling down her cheek. "John had a good heart."

"Indigo murdered that crown prince," Mack pointed out.

Charlie glared. "He grabbed her first. She was defending herself. The prince didn't deserve to live after what he'd done to those poor girls."

"I think I recall the reports on television." Declan's lip twisted. "They said the Saudi crown prince had been killed in a mugging."

Charlie turned the page and kept reading. "I can hear John speaking these words." Another tear rolled down her cheek. "He only wanted to help."

Gus stared at all the images on the monitors and then turned to Jane. Had she been one of the young children who'd gone missing from foster care? Had they beaten her and trained her to be an assassin?

Jane stood back from the others, her face pale, her eyes wide. She stared at the images in front of her, her eyes darting back and forth from one to the next. Her hands shook and her body trembled. Then she looked into Gus's eyes, her own dark with whatever was going through her mind.

"What's wrong?" Gus crossed to her and tried to take her into his arms.

She held up her hand and shook her head. "Don't touch me," she whispered.

Her entire body shook and she wrapped her arms around her middle as if in pain. "I remember," she said. "I *am* Indigo."

As SHE'D STOOD staring at the videos and photos of the girls and boys being indoctrinated into the Trinity Syndicate, something had happened. The iron gate that had been closed for all those weeks due to her beatings and torture opened and a flood of memories washed in. She remembered being taken from the front yard of the foster home where she'd been placed only days after her parents had died in a plane crash. She hadn't even had time to get used to the family that had taken her in when she'd been thrown in the back of a van and taken far away to a training camp in the woods.

She couldn't even tell anyone where the camp was located. She hadn't been able to see out of the van as it traveled for miles along endless highways and then dirt roads, coming to a stop in a place with ramshackle huts and outhouses instead of toilets. All bathing and laundry was done in the nearby frigid stream. She wasn't allowed to speak to anyone without getting hit in the side of the head by some heavy-handed instructor.

The newest recruits slept on dirt floors with only scratchy and threadbare wool blankets to keep them warm. As they graduated from one section of training into another, and they proved themselves worthy, they got army cots or wooden bunks. If they didn't prove themselves strong, fast or smart enough, they were beaten.

The physical demands had been hard, but she'd managed to build her strength and stamina. Along with that, she'd learned never to show emotion.

From the beginning, she'd demonstrated an aptitude for languages. Her trainers sent her straight into Russian and Arabic language training. All of her instruction from then on out had been using these languages only.

Once she'd surpassed her instructors, they turned her to teaching the others until they deemed her ready to deploy.

Her first assignment had been as John's journal had depicted. She'd studied the Saudi crown prince's dossier. He was a piece of work. Not only did he rape young girls, he systematically eliminated anyone in his cabinet who dared to disagree with him. He'd married ten times. When he tired of a wife, he had her killed.

Thankfully, her first assignment was to kill a man who deserved to die.

She'd been given the information on when he would arrive and depart the brothel. She'd wanted to dispatch him before he entered, but he'd arrived earlier than expected. Forced to wait, she practiced her attempt at street girl seduction. Never having flirted in her life, she wasn't very good at it. It didn't matter to the prince. Anything with breasts was fair game. He'd grabbed, she'd punched and the bodyguards had gone down smoothly. Her orders had been to leave at that point. With the prince dead, she'd nailed her first kill.

But she couldn't leave, knowing there were young girls inside the brothel being held against their will. She'd known she'd catch grief if word got back to her handler that she'd gone in. She hadn't cared. This was something she had to do. It was easier to ask forgiveness than for permission.

Her stomach roiled at the memories of the inside of the brothel. The stench of fear and urine filled her nostrils. Images of angry men and screaming girls raced through her mind. She remembered going into that brothel. Remembered taking down the men who'd chained those women to the beds or dosed them heavily with drugs. Rage had burned through her when she'd found the girl who couldn't have been more than eleven years old, beaten and drugged into a coma.

How could these men do this to them? Why wasn't anyone stopping them?

So, she did.

"Jane?" Gus touched her arm. "Are you okay?"

She flinched. "Don't touch me," she said. "I'm exactly what I hoped I wasn't. An assassin. I shouldn't be here. With my kill record, I could spend the rest of my life in prison."

"How many?" Gus asked, then held up his hand. "I don't want to know. Like you said, who you were isn't who you are now."

"Do you remember how you knew my husband?" Charlie asked, clutching the journal close to her chest.

Jane closed her eyes, recalling the day John Halverson had come into her life. She'd been assigned the task of killing a man who'd turned in a Russian sleeper spy who was then sent back to Russia and executed for failing in his mission.

The Russian president had hired Trinity to find and kill the man who'd forced him to eliminate a spy in one of the best positions he could be, as an American government employee of the CIA. He'd had top secret clearances and access to all the data the Russians needed to know exactly what the US was up to almost before mission personnel knew what was going to happen.

Jane had been sent to kill the man who'd lived in the house next door. He was a history professor at a local university.

When Jane had arrived at the man's house, she had disguised herself as a jogger.

Her mark routinely arrived home at a specific

hour and walked from where he parked his car on the street up the sidewalk to his front door.

Jane had faked a fall in front of him. All she had to do was stick the syringe of arsenic into his neck, get up and keep jogging.

But the sound of a little girl's voice made her hesitate.

The front door had opened on the man's house and a little girl of four or five years old smiled broadly and cried out, "Daddy!"

The professor helped Indigo to her feet and turned to scoop his little girl up into his arms. "Hi, sweetie pie. How's my best girl?"

Jane hadn't been able to breathe, much less jab the needle into his neck. He'd called his little girl the same thing her father had called her when he'd come home from work. After all those years of suppressing memories that hurt, they all came back to her, reminding her of how it had been before her parents passed.

She'd looked at the man and his little girl, thanked him for helping her and jogged away. She would have kept running, but a man stepped in her path.

"I met John Halverson after an aborted attempt at an assassination."

"Aborted?" Gus asked.

She nodded. "I couldn't pull the trigger. Or the plunger, in this case." She twisted her lips in a wry smile. "John was there. He'd seen what happened and offered me an alternative to working for Trinity."

"What was the alternative?" Gus asked.

She lifted her chin, her eyes narrowing. "He wanted me to help him bring Trinity down. He said that if I helped him, he'd help me to start over with a new identity, and a new life. I wouldn't have to kill anyone else. I could start over." She shook her head. "I should have known it wouldn't be that easy. But after I didn't hit my mark, I knew I would be in trouble with Trinity. My days would be numbered. He told me no matter what, whether I helped him or not, he'd set me up in my new life. He gave me the coordinates of his home as a measure of his trust in me. If I was ever in trouble, all I had to do was go to him and he'd help me out."

"What did he want you to do for him?" Charlie asked.

"He asked me if I'd be willing to go back to Trinity and find out who was in charge."

Gus cursed. "And you agreed?"

She nodded. "It meant continuing to help them in their efforts to disrupt the world political arena. By the time I met John, I was ready to do whatever it took to stop Trinity from ruining young girls' and boys' lives."

"How did you end up in Syria?" Declan asked.

Jane closed her eyes for a moment. "I hadn't heard from John in a few weeks. He usually sent me encrypted texts from his burner phone to my burner phone. That way neither one of them could be traced back to the owner." She drew in a breath and continued. "It had been a couple of weeks. I had been out of the country in Germany doing some intel gathering for Trinity when I received a text from John."

Charlie frowned. "How long ago was this?"

"Four weeks, I think," Jane responded.

Charlie shook her head. "My husband was murdered four months ago."

Jane frowned. "I got the text from his burner phone number."

"Someone else sent it," Gus said, his gut knotting. There were too many twists and turns in Jane's tale for his comfort.

"He wanted me to get in on a mission to Syria. Trinity was going to assassinate a high-ranking Russian general. John…or whoever…wanted me there to get the general out. He said this would be the last time I'd appear to work for Trinity. After that mission, he'd insist on me leaving the syndicate." She gave a tight smile. "All I had to do was get the general out alive. I was in the right place at the right time with Trinity to be assigned to the mission in Syria. They tasked me to kill the very general I was to save."

"We all heard the news," Gus said. "If you're talking about Marouchevsky, he was supposedly killed when the US bombed the Shayrat airbase."

"That's what they reported." Jane shook her head. "I was there." She raised her hand. "I didn't kill him, but someone else did. Apparently, Trinity was onto me. The person who assassinated the general came after me. I got away from him. Unfortunately, I got too close to the bombing. I must have been knocked unconscious, because when I woke, I was in a cell being interrogated by Russians who'd been working with the Syrian rebels. They wanted to know who had called for the evacuation of the Russian planes but didn't call for *their* evacuation."

"I take it someone from the US gave the Russians a heads-up that Shayrat was about to be bombed," Declan said. "That gave them plenty of time to get their planes out."

Gus didn't like that Jane had been a major pawn in a deadly game. "Funny how our enemies know more about our secrets than we do."

"The general was a double agent for the US and Russia. I'm not sure what kind of deal he worked out with the US, but he was supposed to be evacuated out of Syria to the US. I was supposed to be on the transport with him." Jane sighed heavily. "Neither one of us caught our ride."

"The Senate is conducting an inquiry about that bombing," Cole said.

"When?"

Cole pressed his lips together and stared off into a corner. "I don't remember exactly. I saw it on the internet in passing when I was working at getting into the Dark Web. It's either tomorrow or the next day. Whichever, it's soon."

Charlie yawned, covering her mouth. "It's getting late. I fear I'm losing focus, and others might be, as well. We have what we need for now. Let's call it a night and pick up where we left off in the morning."

Gus started for the stairs leading out of the basement conference room. When Jane didn't follow, he turned back.

"Aren't you afraid I'll be a problem?" Jane asked.

Charlie smiled and yawned again. "If my husband trusted you, I trust you." She patted Jane's cheek. "However, I do want to find out who sent you on that last mission. It wasn't John. Someone else must have John's burner phone. I want to know who that is." She dipped her head toward the people in the room. "I trust you all will have a good night. We have a lot of work to do tomorrow. Though we know Jane is Indigo, we still don't know who she was before Trinity. I believe we owe her a real name, not a code name." She smiled. "Good night."

Jane's gaze followed Charlie up the stairs. As she passed Gus, Jane captured his glance.

Gus held out his hand. He didn't give a damn what the others thought. He wanted Jane to know he was there to protect her.

She placed her hand in his.

He chuckled as he started up the steps out of the basement. "You're not going to argue?"

"I'm too tired to care what anyone thinks." She let him hold her hand all the way up the stairs to the third floor.

Inside the suite, Gus didn't even push the sofa up against the door. He left it in the middle of the room.

Jane's brow twisted. "Do you *want* me to make a break for it? Or are you showing me that you trust me to stay?"

"Like you, I'm tired. I don't think either one of us is leaving this suite until morning." He drew her into his arms and tipped her chin up. "And if you feel like you need to run, by all means. But I, for one, would rather you stayed."

At his words, warmth spread through her body. "And the others?"

"I can't speak for them, but Charlie likes you," Gus said. "And she's the boss." He bent to brush his lips across her forehead. "I'm sorry you had to go through everything you did."

"I don't need anyone's pity," she protested. At the same time, she liked what his lips were doing to her face and wished he would drop a little lower to claim hers.

"So, what do I call you?" Gus swept his lips along her left cheek to capture her earlobe between his teeth.

"Not Indigo. I'm done with Trinity."

"What about Trinity being like the mob? Once you're in, you can never leave."

She snorted. "Oh, I'm sure I can leave…in a body bag."

He pressed a finger to her lips. "Don't."

She looked up into his eyes. "Trinity plays for keeps. As much as I'd like to think I can start over with a new identity and new life, until Trinity is eradicated, and the leader is jailed or killed, I will never be free."

"You don't know what can happen." He bent to claim her lips in what should have been a long, toe-curling kiss. When he brought his head up, he frowned down at her. "Something wrong?"

"You deserve better," she said.

"You're right. So, kiss me again."

When he lowered his head to do just that, she put her hand between his mouth and hers. "Why get mixed up with someone like me when you can have your choice of available, uncomplicated women?"

"I think I'm attracted to complicated." Again, he tried to kiss her.

She pressed her hands against his chest. "You're making it hard for me to resist."

"Then don't." He kissed the tip of her nose. "Unless you don't want to make love with me. In that case tell me now and I'll walk away." He waited for her to do that.

Jane hesitated. He was a good man. She was tainted with a questionable past. He deserved so much better.

Gus dropped his hands to his sides. "I don't want to pressure you into anything you don't want to do."

Knowing it might be the last time she had a chance to be with Gus, Jane didn't want to miss this opportunity. No longer able to fight the desire, she grabbed both sides of his face between the palms of her hands. "Oh, shut up and make love to me."

GUS GATHERED HER in an embrace and pulled her close. "Demanding female, aren't you?" Every part of his body had lit on fire the moment they walked through the door of the suite.

Yes, they'd learned Jane was the assassin Indigo. He should be keeping his distance and watching her even more closely than ever before. But he couldn't resist her. She was strong, determined and sexy as hell. Everything about her screamed *lethal*, yet Gus couldn't fight what was happening inside himself.

He'd never met a woman like Jane. She'd been through so much, and emerged fighting. They had so much more in common than he could have originally guessed. They both were from similar backgrounds, having lost their parents when they were young. They had been through tough combat training and both seen action, killed people and been shot at on more than one occasion.

Post-traumatic stress disorder was a way of life. One they dealt with on a daily basis from all they'd lived through.

From what he'd learned about her in the very short time he'd known Jane, she wanted roots, a place to call home and a family to welcome her there. She'd fit in easily with the team and taken to Charlie's hospitality. He understood that feeling.

For years, Gus thought himself immune to the desire to marry, to have a family of his own. His family was his team. He'd convinced himself it was enough.

Now, with Jane in his arms, he realized he wanted so much more. But why this woman? She wasn't kidding when she said she was complicated. A known assassin, she would find it hard to start over. Being a part of Trinity would make it even harder.

At that moment, all of those thoughts were pushed to the back of his mind as he held Jane in his arms, kissing her and feeling her warm body against his.

She was who he wanted. No matter how hard it would be to extricate her from the tentacles of the Trinity Syndicate, he would do it.

He bent and scooped her up into his arms.

Jane frowned. "Aren't you afraid you'll rip the stitches in your arm?"

Gus shook his head. "I'm more afraid that if I don't get a move on, you'll wise up and change your mind."

She brushed her lips across his. "Not a chance."

Gus carried her into the bedroom and let her slide down his body until her feet touched the ground. Then he backed her up until she bumped into the bed.

"Before we go any further, I want to be perfectly clear. You're all in on this, right?"

She frowned, tipping her head to the side slightly. "I told you to shut up and make love to me. What part of that confused you?"

"Nothing. It's just that I watched you take down two guys in under a minute. I want to be sure you're not going to do the same to me." He winked.

Jane's eyebrows rose. "Is that so?"

He nodded and bent to nuzzle her neck. "You

never know when a woman's going to kick your butt."

"You are so right." Jane grabbed the front of his shirt, spun around and pushed him backward.

Gus landed on the bed, bringing Jane with him.

She landed on top of him with a grunt.

"You didn't have to get all tough on me," Gus said. "I was working my way to this exact position. If you wanted me to move faster, all you had to do was say so."

"You talk too much, marine." Jane lowered her mouth to his, stemming the flow of words from his lips.

"Mmm." She moaned. "This is more like it."

He cupped the back of her head and pulled her closer against him. "Agreed." Then as quickly as she'd toppled him into the bed, he flipped her onto her back and kissed her more fiercely. "I've wanted to do that since I saw you standing in that ballroom in that black dress."

"A stranger? You wanted to kiss a woman you didn't trust?"

"I felt something I hadn't felt in a long time." He looked up at her. "No…that's not right. I felt something I'd never felt before." Gus cupped her face in his hand. "You made me feel. My heart was pumping, my blood flowing hot and fast through my veins. I think that's why I noticed you in the first place. You looked amazing in that dress with your long black hair hanging down around your shoulders."

"I've never had a man talk to me the way you do."

"Then you've never had a man as intrigued as I am." He kissed a path from her earlobe along the side of her jaw to capture her mouth in a searing kiss. "You make me burn inside," he murmured.

She chuckled. "That doesn't sound comfortable."

"There's nothing comfortable about the way I feel about you. I want you so much it hurts."

"Then what are you waiting on?"

"I want you to be sure this is what you want," he said and trailed his lips down the length of her throat to the pulse beating wildly at the base.

"It is what I want. You. Me. Let's make love like there will be no tomorrow. We don't know what's going to happen. We can have tonight at the very least."

She entwined her hands behind the back of his neck and pulled him down to kiss her.

He leaned up on his elbows and stared down into her face. "Why are you so damned beautiful?"

She blinked up at him. "For an assassin?"

Gus frowned. "I didn't say that." He brushed a strand of her hair back behind her ear. "The combination of black hair, smooth skin and brown-black eyes give you an air of mystery I would think most men couldn't resist."

"Apparently, you're the only one who couldn't resist. Most men don't look twice at me."

"Oh, darlin', that's where you're wrong. You are stunningly attractive. I couldn't take my eyes off you at the gala."

"Because you were worried I was going to kill or kidnap Charlie." She shook her head. "I'm just a woman with a load of personal baggage that will make it hard for any man to get close to."

"But you're letting me close," he reminded her.

"Only because I know it won't last. As soon as everyone else figures out that I'm an assassin, one of a couple things could happen."

"Oh really?" He cocked an eyebrow. "What?"

"I'll be hauled off to jail for murder."

"Who will turn you in?" He pressed a kiss to her temple.

"The CIA knows I'm an assassin. When they find me, they'll arrest me, toss me in jail and throw away the key."

Gus captured her earlobe between his teeth and nibbled gently. "I didn't hear Mack or Snow say anything about the evidence that you killed anyone."

"It would only be a matter of time until someone figured it out," she said.

"They haven't so far," Gus said. "What else have you got?"

"Trinity will come after me and make my life miserable until they finally off me with a bullet to the head."

Gus swept his lips across her cheekbone and hovered over her mouth. "Maybe. But I'm not ready to let them through to do the job."

Jane leaned in and brushed her mouth across his. "You might not have a choice. They have a tendency to wait until their victims are convinced they aren't really going to come after them. That's when they strike, swift and deadly. Now, are you done talking, because I can think of better things to do in bed."

Gus kissed a path from her lips over her chin and down the long, sweet length of her neck. "You're right. There are a lot better things to do than talk about Trinity and the CIA." He reached the hollow near her collarbone and paused with his mouth to explore her lower regions with his hands.

He slipped his palm over her thigh and upward to capture her hip and pull her up against his growing erection. Holy hell, he was on fire.

No longer able to resist, he pushed the hem of her shirt up over her torso.

Jane raised her arms and let him tug it over her head.

He tossed it aside and dropped his head, pressing his lips to the swells of her breasts. She smelled of roses or some kind of flowers. He didn't know, but he liked it and tasted her skin with the tip of his tongue. Then he hooked the straps of her bra in his fingers and dragged them down over her shoulders.

Her brow furrowed and she reached behind her, undoing the clasp in the back, freeing herself from the lacy confines.

Pushing it aside he feasted his gaze on her rosy nipples, puckered tightly into pretty little nubs.

Jane clasped her hands behind his head and brought him down to take them into his mouth where he rolled the tight little buttons around with his teeth.

Her back arched off the bed and a low moan left her lips. She gripped the fabric of his shirt and pulled, dragging it over his head.

Restraint flew out the window. Gus stood, took Jane's hand and stood her on her feet. Within seconds, the rest of their clothes ended up on the floor. They stood before each other, naked.

Blood rushed through Gus's veins, pushing adrenaline and desire throughout his body. He wasn't sure what tomorrow would bring, but tonight, she was his.

JANE CUPPED GUS's cheek in her hand and leaned up on her toes to press her lips to his. "I don't know what will happen in the future, but we have now. Let's not waste the time we have."

He wrapped his arms around her waist and dragged her body against his. "I was just thinking the same thing." Gus touched the top of her head with his lips and then pressed kisses to each eyelid.

The pressure was so soft, it took her breath away. With her breasts pressed to the hard muscles of his chest and his erection nudging against her belly, she couldn't think past what he was doing to her. She wanted so much more, but she wanted more to explore every part of his body. When he started to back her into the side of the bed, she shook her head. "Not yet."

Gus groaned. "You're killing me, assassin."

She chuckled. "I've only just begun." Kiss by kiss, she worked her way from his chin, down his neck to the hard ridge of his collarbone. Her fingers traced a path downward, stopping to lightly pinch his hard, brown nipples. She replaced her fingers with her lips, rolling the little buds between her teeth.

Jane inhaled the scent of him, all woodsy and musky male. She wanted to remember that scent for when he wasn't there.

Slowly, she moved downward, dropping to her knees, nipping his skin and licking a path down his torso to the hair at the juncture of his thighs.

Gus threaded his hands into her hair and pulled her closer.

She took him into her mouth, licking the tip of his erection. Then she gripped his buttocks in both palms and pulled him into her.

He sucked in a deep breath and held it, his body stiff, his fingers digging into her scalp.

Jane moved him back out and back in, establishing a slow, sensuous pace, taking him all the way in, until he bumped against the back of her throat. She liked how he tasted, how big he was and how quickly he settled into the rhythm. But she liked even more how much power she had over him. How she turned him on by just being with him.

His thrusts grew faster and she held tight, determined to bring him all the way.

Gus stopped suddenly and pulled free of her mouth, dragged her to her feet and kissed her hard. "I want you where I am."

"I'm almost there," she whispered, her voice ragged, her breathing coming fast.

He shook his head. "You're not even close." He lifted her and laid her on the bed, her legs dangling over the side. Then he parted her thighs and bent down to capture her mouth in a long, satisfying kiss. "You taste of me. You don't know how sexy that is."

She moaned. "I have a good idea. Please, don't

take too long. I'm hot all over and I want you inside me."

"Soon," he said and started his assault on her
senses, by kissing a path from her chin to the base
of her throat where the pulse beat fast. He moved
to take one of her breasts in his mouth, sucking
hard, tonguing her nipple until she arched off the
bed, a moan sounding from deep inside. "Please."

"Soon," he repeated. His hands moved lower,
cupping her sex in his palm.

Jane's breath caught in her throat and hitched
when he pressed a finger into her channel. "Yes!"

He chuckled. "Like that?"

"Yes," she repeated.

His mouth moved over her belly and downward
to the puff of curls covering her sex. He parted
her folds and slipped his tongue over that nub-
bin of flesh packed with a million nerves all firing at once.

Jane gripped his hair in her hands and held him
there, urging him to take more.

He did, tonguing her there until she writhed
against him. "I can't take much more. Please."

He sucked her between his teeth and flicked her
with his tongue until she rocketed over the edge.

Jane tensed, her body tingling from the point of
contact all the way out to the tips of her fingers.
She rode the wave of her release all the way to the

very end, finally dropping back to the bed. Then she dragged him by the hair up her body.

"I need you. Inside me. Now," she said, her voice sounding like a runner having completed a marathon.

Gus scooted her up onto the bed, parted her legs with his knee and slid between them, his erection pressing against her entrance. "Now you're ready."

She smiled up at him. "Oh, yes."

He slid in, filling her channel with his wide girth, pressing in slowly.

Impatient to have all of him, Jane gripped his buttocks and slammed him home.

Gus stayed deep, letting her adjust to his size. Then he slid out, and back in, establishing a rhythm as old as time.

Jane dug her heels into the mattress and lifted up, meeting him thrust for thrust.

His pace increased until he was pumping in and out, again and again. One last thrust and he buried himself deep inside her, his shaft throbbing, his face tight.

Then he collapsed on top of her, took her in his arms and rolled them onto their sides, retaining the connection. He held her close, kissing the top of her head.

"You're amazing," he whispered against her hair.

"I don't want this night to end," she said.

"Me either."

Jane lay in the warmth of his arms long into the night, memorizing each breath he took, wanting to remember everything about this man and their short time together. Tomorrow would come all too soon.

Chapter Twelve

Gus lay awake long into the wee hours of the morning, sexually sated, physically content and wishing the night could go on forever. He wished he could have protected Jane from everything the world had thrown her way. Losing her parents had been bad enough. He knew the pain of loss and the homesickness and terror of leaving everything you ever knew behind you to go into foster care.

But to be taken even from foster care into the harsh reality of a terrorist training camp...

His arm tightened around her. If only he could protect her from how the world would treat her should they discover all she'd done as a trained assassin. He'd bet she'd chafe at his need to protect. She was more than capable of defending herself. If it came down to it, she'd drop out of sight and start a new life somewhere else. More than likely, she'd be on the run from Trinity for the rest of her existence. Organizations like Trinity didn't let their disciples walk away. If they wanted to leave, they were carried away in body bags, as she'd already pointed out.

Like John Halverson, Gus wanted to put a stop to Trinity. Once and for all.

John had made a start at identifying the key players, but he didn't get far. Code names weren't enough. They needed real names, addresses, locations of the handlers to reach the head of the snake. Cut off the head and the snake would die.

Until they found the key players, Jane would remain a target. She would not be at peace unless one of two things happened. The asp was captured…or Jane died.

Though Gus hadn't known Jane for long, he felt a connection that transcended time. They'd suffered similar events and survived. They'd not only survived, they'd grown stronger and more powerful through their adversity.

Gus admired Jane's passionate nature. Not only did she display it in bed, but she displayed it in her willingness to disobey orders to save young girls who had no one else to defend them. She was zealous about her belief that they should live free of their captors.

Sometime in the early morning hours, Gus slept, retaining his hold on the woman who was quickly capturing his heart.

A loud knock on the suite door jerked him out of a dreamless sleep and into an upright position.

The knocking continued.

Gus leaped out of bed and ran naked across the floor to the suite door.

"Gus!" Declan's voice sounded through the paneling. "You awake?"

"I am now." He opened the door a crack and peered into Declan's clean-shaven face. "What's up?"

"Get dressed and meet us in the conference room." Declan didn't give him any more information than that. And from his tone, he wanted him there ASAP.

Gus closed the door and headed for his duffel bag in the other bedroom.

"What's wrong?" Jane asked.

He turned to find her wrapped in a sheet, her hair rumpled and her brow furrowed.

Gus's heart squeezed hard in his chest. He didn't see in her the trained assassin. He saw the beautiful, vulnerable woman. He held his arms open.

She didn't hesitate but fell into them and let him hold her tight.

"Is it that bad?" she murmured against his chest.

Gus chuckled. "I have no idea. I just wanted to hold you." He kissed the top of her head. "He wants us down in the conference room ASAP. We need to get dressed."

"That might be a good idea, considering we're naked." She leaned back and kissed his prickly chin.

"I don't think he meant for me to take time to shave."

"I'm not complaining," she said and kissed his stubbled chin again.

Gus heaved a heavy sigh. "As much as I'd love to blow off Declan, we'd better get moving."

Jane stepped away, dropped the sheet and walked back to the bedroom. "I'll be ready in less than a minute."

With a growl at her blatant temptation, Gus turned back to his duffel bag and pulled out jeans and a T-shirt. He had both on and was shoving his feet into his boots when Jane appeared in his doorway, dressed, her hair neatly brushed and shoes on her feet.

"I don't know any other woman who is that quick to get ready."

"We learned to be fast or be hit."

Gus's fists clenched. He wished he could find the people who'd been Jane's so-called instructors and beat them to a pulp for what they'd done to Jane and their other conscripted assassins.

Moments later, they were descending into the basement conference room where Declan, Cole, Jonah, Charlie and Grace stood around the bank of monitors.

"What's going on?" Gus asked.

"Cole got a tip we need to follow up on." Declan nodded toward one of the monitors with a picture of several men in suits entering a hotel.

"I got an encoded message from the Dark Web early this morning while I was surfing for more information about the bombing in Syria that Jane was involved in." He clicked the keyboard and brought up the words.

Trinity's next mark.

Gus shook his head. "What's that supposed to mean?"

"The message was accompanied with a link to images on the DC news station." Cole pointed to the monitor where the suited men were entering a hotel. The caption beneath the image read *Inquiry into Shayat Airbase Bombing Continues.*

"Isn't that the Willard hotel?" Charlie asked.

Cole nodded. "They're using the conference center in the hotel to conduct the preliminary hearings."

"What kind of security are they employing?" Gus asked.

"A mix of Homeland Security personnel and rent-a-cops." Cole's lip curled. "Apparently, they don't expect it to be a big deal, since it's a preliminary hearing."

"Anyone could access the hotel during the meeting," Declan pointed out.

Charlie tapped a finger to her chin. "They'll probably have the meeting rooms cordoned off, but the rest of the hotel will still be open to guests."

"Do you think you'd recognize any of your fellow assassins if you saw them?" Declan asked Jane.

She shrugged. "Only if they came up through the training with me. And even then, we also trained in disguising ourselves."

A soft ding sounded from the computer.

Cole leaned over the keyboard and clicked a few keys.

Another message popped up.

For more information report to HI HQ, J. Halverson's office.

Charlie gasped. "What the hell? Ask him why."

Cole keyed in the question mark and lifted his hands off the keyboard, waiting.

A full two minutes passed, and no response came.

"I assume HI HQ is the Halverson International building," Declan said.

Charlie nodded, her face pale. "I know it's not John, but if not him, who would have sent that message?"

Cole shook his head. "That's the power of the Dark Web. If you don't want anyone to know who's sending the messages, you can get around the traceability."

"Do you think it's a setup?" Gus asked.

"Halverson International has pretty tight security," Charlie insisted.

"Security can be bypassed," Declan reminded her.

"But we have to go," Charlie insisted. "If this request has anything to do with stopping Trinity from hitting their next mark, we have to respond."

"Then we go." Declan lifted his cell phone to his ear and called Mack. He explained the situation to him. "Get Snow and Mustang on the horn and let them know we're meeting at the Halverson International building as soon as you can get there." He ended the call and nodded toward Jane. "What are we going to do with you?"

Jane's lips twisted. "I'd have booted me off the estate a long time ago."

"Yeah, but we kind of like the way you operate," Declan said. "Minus the assassin thing. Besides, now that you're getting your memory back, you might come in handy identifying fellow Trinity operatives."

Jane nodded. "I'll help in any way I can. However, once we complete training, we're separated from other operatives, so we don't know each other. We don't even see the faces of our handlers. All we have is a cell phone to communicate assignments. Otherwise we're on our own."

"How did you travel in and out of the country?" Declan asked.

"With each assignment, we were given the proper identification documents we'd need. Forged, of course."

"Who gave you the documents?" Gus asked.

"My handler gave me mine," Jane said.

"Could you pick him out in a lineup?" Declan asked. "If Cole finds some shots of Trinity people, do you think you would recognize him?"

Jane shook her head. "Like I said, they never let us see them. Mine always met me in a dark alley with a hat that shadowed his entire face. The only thing I'd have to go on is his voice. That's why it was so hard for Mr. Halverson to fill in the blanks on the chain of command. They guard the levels carefully. I think some are in high-level government positions. I've heard of operatives being killed who learned who their handlers were."

"Sweet heaven, Jane. If it was that dangerous, why did you agree to help John find yours?" Charlie asked.

Jane's jaw firmed. "I didn't want to be a part of an organization that killed innocent women and children."

Grace touched a hand to her lips. "They did that?"

"One of the operatives had a family. To punish him, they murdered his wife and child, in front of him. Then they killed him." Jane's gaze went to Gus. "They sent out a video of what they'd done to all the operatives as a warning. That happened right before John approached me with his request."

"That's awful," Grace whispered.

"All the more reason for me to leave now before they think you all are important to me," Jane said. "I don't want what happened to that man's wife and child to happen to you."

Gus's gut clenched. Jane would have to die for Trinity to leave her alone. He couldn't let that happen. There had to be another way. He wasn't ready to let go of this amazing woman he'd just found.

JANE WAS SURPRISED Charlie wanted her to come with them to Halverson International Headquarters. She suspected it was that *keeping the enemy close* mind-set. She was glad she could accompany them. In a way, she felt responsible for what Trinity was doing. Having been a part of the organization for so long, she'd done things she wished she hadn't. She'd rationalized about the men she'd killed. They'd been bad, having murdered innocent people. Taking them out had been a blessing to others who might have been their next targets.

The rest of the team met up with Charlie and the group from the estate in the garage and went through security and straight up to John Halverson's office.

Margaret met them again at the elevator, a smile on her face. "I'm so glad you came in today. There's an envelope for you. I thought I might have to bring it out to your house."

Charlie patted the woman's arm. "That's not necessary. Just let me know about things and I'll come to the office."

"Yes, ma'am." She handed her the envelope and looked to the others. "Can I get you something to drink?"

The woman reminded Jane of every grandmother she'd ever seen on television. Not that she appeared that old, but that she wanted to help and please the people she considered family or friends.

"No, thank you, Margaret," Declan said for the group.

"We'll be in John's office and we're not to be disturbed," Charlie said, leading the way into the corner office, the envelope in her hand.

Once they were all inside the office, Charlie looked around. "Now what? Are you certain your contact on the Dark Web said we should meet here? Was there a time associated?"

Jane wandered around the office, looking for clues and finding none. She stopped by the floor-to-ceiling windows and stared out at the capitol. The sun was shining, and people were moving about on the streets, happily unaware of the terrorists among them.

Cole lifted his hands, palms upward. "You know as much as I do. We were supposed to get here ASAP."

Gus nodded toward the envelope in Charlie's hand. "What's in the envelope? Maybe it's a message from the Dark Web contact."

Charlie tore open the small white envelope and withdrew a piece of paper. She looked down at it and frowned. "This makes no sense."

She handed the paper to Declan.

The team leader read it aloud. *"Look to the symbol that embodies the strength and stability of our founding father and all shall be revealed."*

The words were typed neatly and centered on the page.

Charlie stared down at the note and shook her head. "What does it mean?"

Jane looked out the window at the skyline. She could barely see the Reflection Pool or the dome of the Capitol Building. The Washington Monument towered over the rest of the buildings, reaching its four-sided obelisk into the blue sky, a testament to the strength and stability of the founding father for which it was named.

Jane's pulse clamored in her veins. "The Washington Monument."

Gus crossed the floor to stand beside her. "What did you say?"

"Read the note again," Jane said, her excitement building.

Declan read aloud again. *"Look to the symbol that embodies the strength and stability of our founding father and all shall be revealed."*

"And who was considered our founding father?" Jane asked, her eyes narrowing as she stared at the towering obelisk.

"George Washington," Charlie answered, stopping to stand beside Jane. "Do you think the note is referring to the Washington Monument?" She stared at the tower. "I don't see anything revealing about it."

"Should we go down there and look?" Declan asked.

"Why don't you look through the telescope?" Gus suggested.

Since Charlie was the closest to the shiny brass telescope, she pressed her eye to the viewfinder and peered through the lens. "I don't see anything different," she murmured.

The whooshing sound of movement made Jane look up.

Blackout shades slid down to cover the floor-to-ceiling windows.

"What the hell?" Gus exclaimed. "Did someone hit a switch?"

"I didn't," Declan said.

"Me, either," Mack added, holding up his hands.

"Something made those shades come down." Charlie backed away from the telescope.

A click and a rumble behind her made Jane turn back to the room's interior. A huge sheet of the wood-paneled wall slid to the side, revealing an array of computer monitors. The one in the center blinked to life, displaying an image of John Halverson.

Jane and Charlie both gasped at the same time.

"I know that face," Jane whispered.

John Halverson gave a sad smile. "Hey, Charlie. If you're viewing this message, I must be gone."

Charlie pressed a hand to her chest; tears welled in her eyes and slid down her cheeks. "Oh, John."

"I had the telescope set up with an optical scanner to read your eyes only. All the security measures I put in place in this room were for a reason. I realized a little too late that what I was getting into could have repercussions that impacted you. I should have told you about it and prepared you for my potential demise."

While John had been talking, Gus grabbed the executive chair from behind the desk and pushed it over to where Charlie stood in front of the video monitor.

She didn't move until Gus touched her shoulder and urged her to sit. Charlie sank into the chair, a soft sob escaping her lips.

"I'd first run across the Trinity Syndicate when

I was working a special project with the CIA. I'm sorry, dear. I knew you didn't want me to get involved in dangerous activities but I couldn't stand by and do nothing when there was an organization out there preying on children and young people, turning them into killing machines for hire and to disrupt the world political arena. I know how much you had wanted children of our own. When that didn't happen, I knew you would have wanted to help other children, like Kate Sanders." John's face disappeared and a photo image of a young girl appeared. She had long, black silky hair and dark brown eyes.

Gus stepped closer. "Is that…?"

"That's Jane," Declan declared.

Gus looked from the image to Jane and back.

John's voice continued. "Kate Sanders's parents died in a plane wreck. With no other family who could take her, she was relegated to foster care. Within days of placing her in a home, she disappeared. The missing children foundation posted her photo on milk cartons, posters, Amber Alerts and the news. She was never found. Until I witnessed a Trinity assassination of a Saudi prince who'd just raped a young girl in a tawdry bordello in New York City."

Jane remembered.

Everything. From the horror of learning she'd lost her parents to the daily beatings during training with Trinity, to when she'd met John Halverson who wanted only to stop Trinity from making monsters out of children.

She was one of Trinity's monsters.

An arm came up around her waist.

She turned to Gus. He didn't say a word, just held her.

"Now that I'm gone," John's voice continued, "you will have a decision to make."

Charlie gave another little sob.

"I never wanted you to be involved in tracking down the handlers and leaders of Trinity. It's dangerous business. You must choose whether to destroy the information I've gathered or pass it on to the FBI or CIA and let them pick up where I left off. I never wanted you to be caught in the repercussions of what I was doing.

"I'm sorry I've left you alone. I know how much you hated it when I was gone. Know this, though, I love you with all my heart."

The video ended and the monitor turned dark.

"When did you say John passed?" Jane asked.

"Four months ago," Charlie said, her voice broken and choked with emotion.

"I was in touch with John via text less than two months ago," Jane whispered. "How can that be?"

"I couldn't let his work die with him," a voice said from a corner of the room.

Jane spun to see Margaret, John's executive assistant, standing near the doorway.

Jane frowned. "You sent me the texts about getting the general out of Shayrat?"

Margaret nodded. "I've worked with John on this project from the beginning. I knew as much, sometimes more than he did. I'm as committed to the downfall of Trinity Syndicate as he was."

"I wish he would have told me," Charlie said.

"He wanted to but felt like he didn't have enough data to be useful. And he wanted to keep you safe. He knew code names of the people in key positions of leadership, but not who the people were behind the codes. When he was murdered, I stepped in where he left off, gathering information. I haven't gotten much further. I'd hoped Indigo would lead to a breakthrough."

"But I failed," Jane said.

"I'm just glad you're alive. I shouldn't have asked you to play the role of a double agent trying to get the Russian general you were supposed to assassinate out of harm's way. Once you did that, I knew I had to find a way to make you disappear. When you failed to go through with your assigned assassinations, Trinity would target you for extermination."

Jane closed her eyes and forced herself to relive that day in Syria, the memories coming back in a collage of images. "The Trinity agent who killed the general came after me." She pinched the bridge of her nose as remembered pain throbbed at the base of her skull. "He knocked me out and left me locked in a building that was supposed to be part of the US airstrike on Shayrat Airbase. I should have died in the attack. Instead, Russians who were working with the Syrian rebels found me and took me to an alternate location to interrogate me."

Gus's arm tightened around her.

"I never learned the identity of my handler. With Trinity, you didn't question, you performed. If you knew too much, it was certain death." She met Margaret's gaze.

"Then why did you agree to help John?" Charlie asked.

Jane's lips twisted. "I was tired of the killing, even though the people Trinity had me go after weren't model citizens, like the Saudi crown prince. I didn't want the syndicate to keep training kids to be like me. And I wanted out."

"And I'm still working on how to get you out and how to keep you safe," Margaret said, looking at Charlie, "as I know John would have wanted. I only bring you in on this now because you've already uncovered so much."

Jane snorted. "By now, you must realize the only way out of Trinity is death."

"No," Gus said. "I refuse to accept that."

"They know I've defected," Jane said. "The attack on the freeway was the first attempt at damage control. There will be others until they tie up this loose end."

"You are not a loose end," Margaret said. "John had a lot of faith in you. I failed you when I sent you in to get the general out."

"What was so important about the general?" Charlie asked. "And how did you get involved with him?"

"John had been working with the CIA in his effort to track down Trinity leaders. The CIA asked for help in return. I picked up where John left off with Indigo. The CIA learned of a leak in military intelligence. Information was getting to the Russians about our military operations. The CIA wanted to know who was leaking that information. The Russian was the CIA's plant. He was there when the Russians received word to evacuate Shayrat. Someone warned them about the pending US strike. The general's cover had been compromised. The CIA wanted to get him out. Indigo was there. She'd sent a message to John that she'd been tasked with the general's assassination, not knowing John had been murdered. The CIA had tapped into the burner phone she used to keep in touch with John. They knew what I knew and asked me to intervene to save the general." Margaret held out her hands, palms up. "I took over when John passed but I need help. I need Declan's Defenders. And I need them now."

"You're my link on the Dark Web, aren't you?" Cole asked.

Margaret nodded. "And I have a situation I need your help to resolve."

"Why didn't you go to the CIA or FBI?" Charlie asked.

"I don't know who to trust anymore. I'm beginning to think Trinity has tentacles in the government. Their leadership might be entrenched somewhere in the CIA, FBI or State Department. I think that's why Indigo's mission to extract the general failed. Someone knew from the inside that she'd defected and sent someone out to make sure the general died as well as Indigo. But that's not why I brought you here." She glanced down at the watch on her wrist. "In three hours, there is a preliminary hearing concerning the bombing at Shayrat. My contacts on the Dark Web indicate there will be an attack on the people in that hearing. They are to spare no one and make it look like a random terrorist attack by ISIS, not a precision execution staged by Trinity."

"What do you want us to do?" Jane asked, knowing before the woman responded.

Margaret's gaze swept the room, pausing to connect with each person, one by one, before she answered. "We need to stop the attack."

Chapter Thirteen

Three hours hadn't been much time to organize, arm and plan their defense.

The hearing had been set up at a posh hotel's conference room center.

Cole had hacked into the hotel's database and secured a reservation for Mr. and Mrs. Walsh arriving that day for a one-night stay. Gus and Jane would enter the hotel with their luggage containing the weapons the team would need to combat the threat.

Cole would man the communications van parked on the street, tap into the hotel's internal security cameras and direct those inside with what he saw.

Mack and Snow would enter the hotel as electric technicians there to fix a problem with a faulty circuit. Cole had already hacked into the hotel's systems to generate the work order.

Mustang and Declan had found their way inside

earlier by sneaking into the back of a delivery van, delivering hotel staff uniforms. They'd snagged a couple of janitor coveralls and slipped through the loading dock entrance into the hotel's laundry facility. From there, they'd work their way inward to the conference center.

Each member of the team and Jane had been equipped with state-of-the-art communications devices John Halverson had stashed in a hidden storeroom in his office. The communications van, according to Margaret, had been a special project he'd been working on before he passed.

Cole had jumped in, booted the computers, updated their software and connected all of the headsets to his dashboard. He was positioned less than a block away from the hotel in a pay-to-park lot.

Gus, dressed in black trousers and a long-sleeve button-down dark shirt, stared across the backseat of the rented limousine at Jane.

She wore a sleek black jumpsuit with a black patent-leather belt cinched around her narrow waist. Charlie had loaned her the outfit, a broad-brimmed black-and-white hat and large dark sunglasses.

Jane had swept her silky black hair high up on her head and tucked it into the hat, exposing her long, sexy neck. In the matching black patent-leather pumps, she looked like a stunning DC socialite.

"What?" she said.

Gus hadn't realized he'd been staring until then. "What what?"

"Do I look all right for the part?" she asked, brushing away an imaginary speck from her pant leg.

"You look amazing," Gus said. "I only hope the Trinity operatives don't recognize you."

"In this outfit, I don't see how they can." Jane's lips twisted. "I don't think I've ever worn anything this fancy."

"All we have to do is get in, set up and then slip down to the lobby. If Trinity is planning a coup by storming the entrance, we'll be the first line of defense with the security guards that will be in place for the hearing."

"And if they plan on a subtler attack, we can watch for infiltration, one at a time."

"Right." He reached for her hand. "I would have preferred for you to stay back with Charlie. You've been through enough already." When she started to frown, he held up his other hand. "I know you're perfectly capable of taking care of yourself. I've just never worked a mission with someone like you."

One side of her mouth curled in a half smile. "An assassin?"

"No. A woman I find myself deeply attracted to." He shook his head. "It must be the male gene.

Every protective instinct in me is screaming for me to shield you from harm."

Jane's brow dipped lower. "Gus, you can't operate that way. You have to treat me like one of your team. You have to know I've got your back just as much as you have mine. You can't be thinking about protecting me when you have a job to do."

He nodded and squeezed her hand. "My mind tells me that, but my heart is freaking out."

She captured his cheeks between her palms and stared into his face, her dark eyes so intense. "Focus, marine." Then she kissed him hard, her mouth taking his by storm.

He pulled her close in the back of the limousine and deepened the kiss until they were both breathless.

The limousine pulled up in front of the hotel and came to a stop.

Jane stared once more into Gus's eyes.

He wanted to kiss her again, but knew the time had come. "Ready?"

She nodded.

He touched the communication headset in his hear. "Cole?"

"Gotcha," Cole said into the earbud communications device in Gus's ear. "Indigo?"

"That's Jane, to you," Jane answered.

Cole chuckled. "I stand corrected. Everyone set?"

Declan, Mustang, Mack, Snow and Arnold all reported in.

"It's game time," Declan said.

Arnold opened the door and held it for Jane.

She slid her legs out the door and let Arnold pull her to her feet.

Gus got out behind her and waited while Arnold unloaded the suitcase filled with the disassembled parts of the weapons they might need if the assault happened as indicated on the Dark Web.

Placing one hand on the small of her back, the other on the handle of the rollaway suitcase, Gus walked with Jane into the hotel. The limousine left the covered entrance and drove away. Arnold would park it in the pay-to-park lot near where Cole had positioned the van. He'd be Cole's eyes around the van and backup for the team inside if the going got tough.

Security guards stopped Gus on the way into the hotel. He showed his identification.

Jane patted her body and looked up at the guards with a grimace. "Oh, dear, I left my purse in the limousine."

"We'll notify the limousine company when we get inside." Gus pointed to the clipboard the security guard held with the names of the guests due to arrive. "That's us there, Mr. and Mrs. Walsh." He prayed the guard wouldn't insist on inspecting the contents of the case. The disassembled weapons were tucked into hidden compartments, but a smart guard would notice the case was bigger than the interior showed, and heavier than the few items displayed inside.

The guard put a check beside Gus's name, nodded and stepped aside, allowing them to enter the lobby.

A number of men wearing business suits stood around, talking in small groups.

Margaret had done her homework and shown them pictures of some of the people who would be attending the preliminary hearing.

Gus recognized a few of the men. "The delegates are here," he said softly.

"All is quiet in the hallways and at the entrances," Cole reported.

Gus and Jane walked to the front desk and registered. A few minutes later, they were in the elevator on their way up to their third-floor room.

"Delegates are making their way to the conference center," Cole reported.

"Almost to our room," Gus said.

They emerged from the elevator and walked to the room, waved the key card over the locking mechanism and they were in.

Gus quickly laid the case on the bed, unzipped it and unfolded it.

While he opened the hidden compartment on one side, Jane uncovered the other side. They quickly assembled the weapons in time for a knock on the door.

Gus checked through the peephole and then opened the door to Declan and Mustang dressed in janitor uniforms.

Wordlessly, Jane supplied them with handguns and several magazines of ammunition.

They tucked the guns in their pockets and exited, headed down the stairwells toward the second floor where the conference rooms were located.

A moment later, Snow and Mack arrived wearing the electrician uniforms.

"Wish I had a submachine gun," Snow lamented.

"Kind of hard to hide one," Gus said and handed Snow several magazines of ammo.

"Let's hope this doesn't get too ugly," Mack said. "There are a lot of guests in the hotel today besides the delegates for the hearing."

"The conference room doors have been closed, all delegates inside," Cole reported into their ears.

"Let's get this show on the road," Snow said. He and Mack left the room and headed down to the opposite end of the hallway where Declan and Mustang had gone and descended the stairwell.

Gus watched until they disappeared and then turned back to Jane. "Ready?"

"Almost." She strapped on a shoulder holster and tucked a handgun in the pocket. Then she slipped on the jacket Charlie had loaned her to go with the black jumpsuit. She pulled the pant leg of her suit up and checked the strap of the scabbard holding the knife she'd chosen to carry. Then she lifted the other pant leg and patted the spare magazine strapped there.

Gus smiled. "All I have to say is that I'm glad you're on our side."

She dropped the pant leg and straightened, her eyes sparkling. "You should be." Then she stepped up to him, planted a kiss on his lips and said, "I'm ready."

He grabbed her around the waist, his hand bumping against the gun beneath her jacket. It didn't deter him from pulling her close and kissing her harder. Then he set her away from him and muttered, "Focus."

"That's right. We have to focus."

Gus opened the door and stepped into the hallway, checking left and right before he held out his hand to Jane.

She placed her fingers in his palm and walked with him to the elevator.

Once inside, Gus pushed the button and waited for the doors to slide shut.

As they closed, Cole's voice sounded in his ear. "We have movement in the hallway from the direction of the kitchen." His voice was tight, urgent.

The elevator door closed all the way and the car started down.

An explosion rocked the building.

The elevator shuddered to a stop and the lights blinked out.

"Damn." Gus pulled his cell phone out of his pocket and turned on the flashlight application. "We're trapped in the elevator. What's going on out there?"

"Can't tell," Cole replied. "The security cameras blinked off. Wait—they're back on and the hallways are lit with emergency lights. It's a lot harder to see anything with them."

"Where are the guys who were coming from the kitchen?"

"Hold on…" Cole said. "There. They're climbing the east stairwell to the second floor. They appear to be carrying automatic weapons."

"Should have brought a submachine gun," Snow said into Gus's ear.

"You guys will have to start the party without us. We're stuck in the elevator. But not for long." Gus laid his phone on the ground, the flashlight pointing up. Then he reached up and pushed on the panel above his head, shoving it to the side.

"Need a boost?" Jane laced her fingers and cupped her hands.

Gus stepped into Jane's palms and pulled himself up through the narrow opening into the elevator shaft. The elevator had stopped five feet below the third floor. If they could open the doors on the third floor, they could get out.

He leaned over the trap door and looked down at Jane's face gazing up at him. "Give me your hand."

She reached up and clasped his hand in hers.

He pulled her up through the hole until she could grasp the edges of the opening and drag herself the rest of the way through. Her hat had been knocked off and her hair spilled out of the pins and down her back. She'd tossed the sunglasses in the dark. This was the woman Gus was growing to love and admire. Not the socialite in the fancy clothing, but the kick-ass female who could take a man down with her hands and her skills.

Together, they dragged the elevator doors open to the third floor.

The hallway was empty, the only illumination that of the emergency lighting and the exits signs.

Gus pulled himself up and out the elevator doors, then reached down and helped Jane up to stand beside him.

No sooner were they on their feet than they were running for the stairwell.

"We're out and moving," Gus reported. "Heading down the west stairwell."

"Beware," Cole said. "More men, heavily armed, are heading up from the ground floor to the second floor. You might converge at the same time."

"Got it," Gus said.

"Looks like they have the conference room on lockdown," Cole added.

Cole pulled the handgun from the shoulder holster beneath his suit jacket and ran down the stairs.

Below him, he could hear the clumping sound of boots coming up the stairs from below.

Halfway down to the second floor, Gus paused on the landing and waited for Jane to catch up. *Ready.* He mouthed the word.

She gave one brief nod.

They descended quietly, clinging to the wall as they rounded to the landing onto the second floor.

Two men, carrying semiautomatic rifles, charged up the stairs only a few steps from the top. They wore black clothes, black ski masks and no police markings on the tactical vests they had strapped on over their shirts.

When the lead man spotted Gus, he jerked his rifle up in front of him and fired.

Gus saw the move coming and backed around the corner, pushing Jane behind him. If the gunmen had been hotel guards or Department of Homeland Security, they would have identified themselves before shooting.

The bullets pounded into the wall where he'd been standing.

He ducked low and popped out around the corner at around knee level and fired, hitting the man in the chest.

The man staggered backward but didn't go down.

Figuring he must be wearing protective armor in his tactical vest, Gus aimed lower and hit him in the knees.

The front man dropped and rolled to the side to be replaced by another.

He fired up the stairs.

Gus lay flat on the floor and returned fire.

Behind him, Jane came out from the corner and aimed at the man's head, hitting him with her first round. The man went down and didn't move.

She fired at the guy Gus had hit in the knee. He didn't move.

Gus and Jane descended the rest of the way to the second floor and pushed open the stairwell door, just enough to look down the hallway.

The sound of gunfire echoed off the walls along with the screams of people caught in the melee.

"Five shooters have made it to the doors of the conference center," Cole said. "Four more are on their way through the lobby."

Jane darted past Gus and ran down the hallway toward the conference center.

"Wait," Gus called out. "You can't go in alone."

"What's going on?" Cole demanded.

"Jane's almost to the corner. She ran ahead."

Gus raced after her, close, but not close enough to cover for her. The woman had worked alone for so long, she didn't know what it meant to wait for backup.

Now she was running straight into a situation where she'd be outnumbered from the get-go.

When Jane disappeared around the corner, Gus's heart skipped several beats. He wasn't far behind her, but any distance could mean the difference between dead and alive.

Shots were fired and the blurp sound of a machine gun made Gus's blood run cold.

He burst out from around the corner to find Jane lying prone on the ground, her handgun in front of her. She fired one round after another until her magazine had emptied. When Jane dropped the magazine, and pulled the second one from the strap on her leg, Gus laid down protective fire, aiming for the man who'd taken cover in an alcove. One man had a submachine gun he aimed around the corner, firing indiscriminately.

"Declan and Mustang have the ground floor," Cole reported. "They're firing now on the men moving through the lobby. Snow and Mack made it into the conference room before the lockdown. They're protecting the doors."

"We've got the hallway in front of the conference room," Jane said.

"No, we don't," Gus disagreed. "There are five

of them and two of us. And one of them is armed with a submachine gun."

"He wasn't carrying additional rounds," Jane said. "He'll blow through what he has soon. We only have to keep him from doing it in the conference room."

The hallway went silent for a moment.

When Gus took the opportunity to duck out from the corner and fire, Jane grabbed hold of his shirt and yanked him back behind cover.

The man with the submachine gun lay in the middle of the hallway, aiming low to the ground. He let loose a burst toward where Jane and Gus were positioned, the number of bullets coming at them chipped away at the corner, spewing Sheetrock dust and paint.

When the firing ceased, Gus dared to look around the corner. The man with the machine gun was gone, along with his backup.

"They're closing in on the conference room," Gus said. "I'm going forward."

Jane jumped up beside him. "Not without me."

Together, they raced after the attackers, rounded another corner and came face-to-face with the five men in black ski masks, all pointing weapons at them.

"Drop your weapons and we might let you live."

"In that case," Gus said. "No." He dove for Jane as the men opened fire.

A bullet hit his arm and one pierced his side.

Jane fell to the floor, crushed by his weight.

The doors to the conference room burst open. Declan and Mustang emerged, firing on the men attacking Jane and Gus.

From the other end of the hallway, Snow and Mack flew out of the stairwell and fired, careful not to hit Declan and Mustang.

Gus lay on top of Jane, holding her down as the others picked off the attackers one by one.

When the shooting stopped, Gus rolled to the side and checked Jane. "Hey, are you all right?" Blood pooled on the floor around them.

"I think I was hit," she said, her voice weak. She reached out and touched near the wound on his shoulder. "I can't tell if it's my blood or yours."

Gus pushed to his feet, pain shooting through his side and arm. He didn't care. Jane had been hit.

He bent and lifted her in his arms. "We have to get you to a hospital."

She shook her head. "No. I don't have any identification. And for all I know, I'm probably on a CIA most wanted list. You can't take me to a hospital. But *you* can go. Put me down."

He shook his head. "You're going." Gus headed for the stairs.

Declan stepped in front of him. "Let me take her. You're hurt."

"No. I've got her," Gus insisted. "Get out of my way. She needs a hospital, ASAP."

Gus had just about reached the stairs when a man burst through the doorway and blocked Gus's path.

"No one leaves Trinity alive," he said and pointed a gun at Jane in Gus's arms.

Jane gasped. "I know that voice."

"You should. You worked for me," the man said in a low, menacing tone. "Since you insist on disobeying orders, Trinity has no more use for you."

Gus, with his hands full, couldn't do anything but hold Jane. If he dropped her, she'd be no better off. Her handler would redirect his aim and kill her anyway.

"Don't hurt her," Gus said. "She might die anyway."

The man shook his ski-mask-covered head. "Can't leave loose ends."

"Maybe so, but I can't let you hurt my people," a woman's voice sounded behind the man.

A shot rang out.

Gus stood for a moment fully expecting the bullet to have hit either him or Jane.

The gun slipped from the hand of the man in front of him and fell to the floor. A second later, the man toppled over, dead.

Margaret Rollins stood behind the dead man, a .45 caliber Glock in her hand. She wore dark pants, a dark shirt and had her hair pulled back in a tight ponytail.

Gus, Jane, Declan and the others all glanced her way, brows raised.

"What? Did you think I was only John's secretary?" She snorted. "Back in my prime, I worked as a field agent for the CIA. I know how to fire one of these." She nodded toward the man on the ground. "Ask him." Then she bent to pull the mask off the man's head and nodded. "I thought we had a leak in Halverson International." Quincy Phishburn lay on the ground at her feet. "And I had an inkling it was him."

"I'd love to stand here and argue but Jane needs a doctor," Gus reminded her.

"I have an ambulance on standby downstairs," Margaret said. "Let one of the others carry her down."

"I'm taking her." Gus stepped around Margaret and descended the stairs to the ground level.

Police, SWAT and emergency medical personnel filled the lobby, caring for the injured and taking statements.

Cole and Arnold had joined them as soon as the threat had been neutralized.

"Lay her down here," an EMT insisted, pointing Gus to a stretcher that had been rolled in from one of the waiting ambulances.

"Get her to a hospital before she loses too much blood," Gus insisted.

"We will. Let us stabilize her before we go too far," the EMT said. "And in the meantime, take a seat on the other stretcher. You're bleeding all over the floor."

Declan placed a hand on Gus's shoulder. "Let them stop your bleeding," he said. "You're of no use to Jane if you die."

Gus eventually stepped back and let the medical personnel work over Jane. Mack and Snow ganged up on him and forced him to take a seat on a stretcher. "Don't leave her for a moment. Trinity might have someone standing by to take her out."

"We'll stick with her," Declan said. "You're losing blood. You need to let the emergency medical team help you."

"Damn it, don't worry about me. See to Jane." Gus fought back the hazy gray fog blurring his vision. "I let her down. I didn't keep her from being shot."

"You did the best you could." Declan patted his arm. "Cole, Mustang, Mack and Snow are standing around Jane. They'll make sure she gets to the hospital and the treatment she needs. You need to go, as well."

The EMTs wheeled Jane to an ambulance first. Four of Declan's Defenders climbed into the ambulance with her. Two in the front, two in the back, making it pretty crowded inside, but reassuring Gus that she would be guarded with their lives if necessary.

"Hurry up. Get me into the ambulance," Gus shouted. "I need to get to the hospital."

Margaret appeared beside him. "I'm going with you to the hospital. I have a proposal we need to discuss. Are you going to be conscious enough to listen?"

Gus closed his eyes for a moment and then nodded, reopening them. "I'm listening. As long as we get to the hospital at the same time as they bring Jane in, I'm all ears." And as long as he didn't pass out from loss of blood.

Margaret climbed into the back of the ambulance after they loaded Gus. They shut the door and pulled out into DC traffic, sirens blaring.

After the EMT situated Gus's IV and hooked up a blood pressure cuff, he sat back and nodded to Margaret.

Margaret leaned close to Gus's ear and laid out her plan.

Chapter Fourteen

"Ashes to ashes, dust to dust," the preacher said as he presided over the memorial service and the scattering of the cremated remains. With a gloved hand, he lifted a small amount of ashes and tossed it into the small hole in the ground where a tree would be planted.

"Jane would have loved that we chose a red-leaf maple tree for her service," Charlie said, wiping a tear from her eye. "She was always so tough on the outside, but I truly believe she was soft on the inside. She only wanted to belong somewhere, to find love."

"She's in a much better place," Declan assured Charlie. "Wouldn't you agree, Gus?"

With a gloved hand, Gus scooped ashes from the urn and dropped them into the hole in the ground. "Yes. I'll miss the black-haired beauty. She taught me a lot about never giving up and always fighting for what you believe in." He stepped back and brushed the ashes from his hands. "Jane Doe, Kate Sanders, rest in peace. You were a fighter and a beautiful soul."

Grace dropped ashes into the hole and murmured, "Rest in peace, Jane."

One by one, the other members of Declan's Defenders all paid their respects to the departed by dropping dirt or ashes into the hole.

"Need help planting her tree?" Declan asked.

Gus stared at the slim sapling. "No. I've got this."

When the last person had gone on to Charlie's place, Gus settled the maple tree into the hole and filled in dirt all around the roots. Then he patted down the dirt, pressing it in with his boot until the tree stood on its own, small, proud and strong. Like Jane.

He sighed, turned and walked to the waiting limousine Charlie had offered for the occasion.

Arnold, Charlie's butler, stood by the door, his shoulders back, his face expressionless. "Ready?" he asked.

Gus nodded. "Back to Charlie's?"

Arnold nodded. "Yes, sir."

"Please, don't call me sir. I work for a living."

"Yes, sir," Arnold said. Was that a twinkle in the older man's eye?

He opened the back door of the limousine and

waited while Gus slid in. Then he closed the door and took his seat behind the steering wheel.

As Gus settled back against the seat a hand slid over his leg. "Was that as strange for you as it was for me?" a smoky voice said.

He turned to the blonde beside him and gathered her into his embrace. "Whatever you do, don't make me bury you twice. Agreed?"

She stared up at him with her blue eyes so different than Jane Doe's dark brown irises and smiled. "I'll do my best to stay alive."

"So, Jasmine, what's your plan?"

"I've been talking with Grace's friend, Emily, who teaches Russian at the local university and does interpretive work on the side. I think I might have a chance at working as an interpreter."

"Are you afraid it will expose you to the people who might recognize you?"

"Not since I have the different hair. Charlie said she'd help me get a different face to go along with my new identity."

"What if I like your face the way it is?" He bent to kiss the tip of her nose.

She tipped her face and captured his mouth with hers. "I guess it all depends on how soon Trinity is brought down," she said.

"We're working on it. Now that Charlie knows what her husband was up to, she's taking it as her challenge to finish what he started."

"Sounds like Declan's Defenders will have their hands full with that task." She cupped his cheeks between her palms. "You have to be careful, though. Trinity plays for keeps. And they won't go down easily."

"I've gathered that. But as long as they're still in operation, you'll never be safe, even with your new hair, eye color and identity. The change is only buying time until we can eliminate the organization." Gus frowned, his jaw tightening. "And we will."

"Though I'll be working as an interpreter by day, you know I'll help in every way I can. I want them stopped even more than John Halverson. Those kids they are taking deserve a better life. Not what Trinity has in store for them."

"Then let's get this mission started, Jasmine Katherine Newman. Charlie, Declan and the others are waiting for us in the conference room. And when we're done with the meeting, we have some catching up to do."

She wrapped her arms around his neck. "Are you sure your injuries are healed enough?"

"I don't care if they are or not. I haven't held you close since your 'death' and your ride to the morgue. Now that the funeral's over, I plan on catching up on lost time."

"Mmm, count me in on that plan. Beats dying any day. And I hope I never to visit another morgue until I am completely dead, not just faking it." And she kissed him, long and hard.

As his tongue swept past her teeth to caress hers, Gus vowed to take down Trinity if it was the last thing he did. This woman deserved to live a happy life, free of fear. Preferably with him. He still found it difficult to believe he'd fallen in love with an assassin. More so, that she'd fallen in love with him.

* * * * *

Get 4 FREE REWARDS!

We'll send you 2 FREE Books plus 2 FREE Mystery Gifts.

Harlequin Intrigue® books feature heroes and heroines that confront and survive danger while finding themselves irresistibly drawn to one another.

FREE Value Over $20

YES! Please send me 2 FREE Harlequin Intrigue® novels and my 2 FREE gifts (gifts are worth about $10 retail). After receiving them, if I don't wish to receive any more books, I can return the shipping statement marked "cancel." If I don't cancel, I will receive 6 brand-new novels every month and be billed just $4.99 each for the regular-print edition or $5.99 each for the larger-print edition in the U.S., or $5.74 each for the regular-print edition or $6.49 each for the larger-print edition in Canada. That's a savings of at least 12% off the cover price! It's quite a bargain! Shipping and handling is just 50¢ per book in the U.S. and $1.25 per book in Canada.* I understand that accepting the 2 free books and gifts places me under no obligation to buy anything. I can always return a shipment and cancel at any time. The free books and gifts are mine to keep no matter what I decide.

Choose one: ☐ **Harlequin Intrigue®**
Regular-Print
(182/382 HDN GNXC)

☐ **Harlequin Intrigue®**
Larger-Print
(199/399 HDN GNXC)

Name (please print)

Address   Apt. #

City   State/Province   Zip/Postal Code

Mail to the **Reader Service:**
IN U.S.A.: P.O. Box 1341, Buffalo, NY 14240-8531
IN CANADA: P.O. Box 603, Fort Erie, Ontario L2A 5X3

Want to try 2 free books from another series? Call 1-800-873-8635 or visit www.ReaderService.com.

---

*Terms and prices subject to change without notice. Prices do not include sales taxes, which will be charged (if applicable) based on your state or country of residence. Canadian residents will be charged applicable taxes. Offer not valid in Quebec. This offer is limited to one order per household. Books received may not be as shown. Not valid for current subscribers to Harlequin Intrigue books. All orders subject to approval. Credit or debit balances in a customer's account(s) may be offset by any other outstanding balance owed by or to the customer. Please allow 4 to 6 weeks for delivery. Offer available while quantities last.

Your Privacy—The Reader Service is committed to protecting your privacy. Our Privacy Policy is available online at www.ReaderService.com or upon request from the Reader Service. We make a portion of our mailing list available to reputable third parties that offer products we believe may interest you. If you prefer that we not exchange your name with third parties, or if you wish to clarify or modify your communication preferences, please visit us at www.ReaderService.com/consumerschoice or write to us at Reader Service Preference Service, P.O. Box 9062, Buffalo, NY 14240-9062. Include your complete name and address.

HI20

"Let's try this again." Logan wiped his dusty palm against his
shirt and held out his hand. "I'm Captain Logan Hess with US
Delta Force."

Her mouth formed an O but at least she took his hand this time
in a firm grip, her skin rough against his. "I'm Lana Moreno, but
you probably already know that, don't you?"

"I sure do." He jerked his thumb over his shoulder. "I saw
your little impromptu news conference about an hour ago."

"But you knew who I was before that. You didn't track me
down to compare cowboy boots." She jabbed him in the chest
with her finger. "Did you know Gilbert?"

"Unfortunately, no." Lana didn't need to know just how
unfortunate that really was. "Let's get out of the dirt and grab
some lunch."

She tilted her head and a swathe of dark hair fell over her
shoulder, covering one eye. The other eye scorched his face.
"Why should I have lunch with you? What do you want from

me? When I heard you were Delta Force, I thought you might have known Gilbert, might've known what happened at that outpost."

"I didn't, but I know of Gilbert and the rest of them, even the assistant ambassador who was at the outpost. I can guarantee I know a lot more about the entire situation than you do from reading that redacted report they grudgingly shared with you."

"You are up-to-date. What are we waiting for?" Her feet scrambled beneath her as she slid up the wall. "If you have any information about the attack in Nigeria, I want to hear it."

"I thought you might." He rose from the ground, towering over her petite frame. He pulled a handkerchief from the inside pocket of his leather jacket and waved it at her. "Take this."

"Thank you." She blew her nose and mopped her face, running a corner of the cloth beneath each eye to clean up her makeup. "I suppose you don't want it back."

"You can wash it for me and return it the next time we meet."

That statement earned him a hard glance from those dark eyes, still sparkling with unshed tears, but he had every intention of seeing Lana Moreno again and again—however many times it took to pick her brain about why she believed there was more to the story than a bunch of Nigerian criminals deciding to attack an embassy outpost. It was a ridiculous cover story if he ever heard one.

About as ridiculous as the story of Major Rex Denver working with terrorists.

Her quest had to be motivated by more than grief over a brother. People didn't stage stunts like she just did in front of a congressman's office based on nothing.

Don't miss
Enemy Infiltration *by Carol Ericson,*
available November 2019 wherever
Harlequin® Intrigue books and ebooks are sold.

www.Harlequin.com

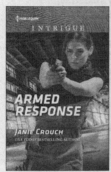

Looking for more satisfying love stories
with community and family at their core?

Check out **Harlequin® Special Edition**
and **Love Inspired®** books!

New books available every month!

CONNECT WITH US AT:

Facebook.com/groups/HarlequinConnection

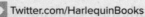 Facebook.com/HarlequinBooks

 Twitter.com/HarlequinBooks

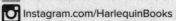 Instagram.com/HarlequinBooks

 Pinterest.com/HarlequinBooks

ReaderService.com

**ROMANCE WHEN
YOU NEED IT**

HFGENRE2018

Love Harlequin romance?

DISCOVER.

Be the first to find out about promotions, news and exclusive content!

Facebook.com/HarlequinBooks

Twitter.com/HarlequinBooks

Instagram.com/HarlequinBooks

Pinterest.com/HarlequinBooks

ReaderService.com

EXPLORE.

Sign up for the Harlequin e-newsletter and download a free book from any series at **TryHarlequin.com.**

CONNECT.

Join our Harlequin community to share your thoughts and connect with other romance readers!
Facebook.com/groups/HarlequinConnection

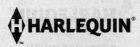

HARLEQUIN®

ROMANCE WHEN YOU NEED IT

HSOCIAL2018